Sue McCauley lives in Christchurch. Her previous work includes four novels — *Other Halves* (1982), *Then Again* (1986), *Bad Music* (1990) and *A Fancy Man* (1996) — a short story collection *It Could Be You* and the non-fiction *Escape From Bosnia — Aza's Story*. Four of these books were shortlisted for the Montana/Wattie Awards and *Other Halves* went on to win both the Wattie Book of the Year Award and the NZ Book Award for fiction. She also writes for stage, screen and radio.

LIFE
ON
EARTH

SUE McCAULEY

v

VINTAGE

Dedication:

for Aunty Rachel, with love.

Acknowledgements:

Heartfelt thanks to Creative New Zealand for faith and funding,

to Harriet Allan for being the publishing editor writers dream of,

to Rachel Scott for keeping me comprehensible, and

to Esther Bunning for the fabulous cover.

 The assistance of Creative New Zealand is
gratefully acknowledged by the publishers.

National Library of New Zealand Cataloguing-in-Publication Data
McCauley, Sue.
Life on earth / Sue McCauley.
ISBN 1-86941-549-3
1. Love stories, New Zealand. I. Title.
NZ823.2—dc 21

A VINTAGE BOOK
published by
Random House New Zealand
18 Poland Road, Glenfield, Auckland, New Zealand
www.randomhouse.co.nz

First published 2003

© 2003 Sue McCauley

The moral rights of the author have been asserted

ISBN 1 86941549 3
Design: Elin Termannsen
Cover design: Esther Bunning
Author photograph: Bruce Foster
Printed in Australia by Griffin Press

CONTENTS

FOOTNOTES

Our bed is a cricket field. You curled in the outfield, me face down on the pitch. I dispatch my foot — a small search party of volunteering toes groping blindly. In a universe of unseen feet, my foot would know your foot.

Once our bed was small with empty margins. We slept as an entity, limbs jointly owned. Your lungs warmed the air I breathed.

Little by little we prised ourselves apart. I became aware of numbness, pins and needles. My hair made you sneeze. One night you turned away, or I did. Whichever, it felt like the first betrayal. But at least on the tip of that iceberg we could breathe freely. Soon parts of us strayed into the cool, clean margins of our bed. We began to think wistfully of being spread-eagled.

In a year of mild opulence we traded in our bed for a regal model: inner-sprung, roll free, orthopaedically approved. We looked at many beds and listened to almost as many bed salesmen and one bed saleswoman. They urged us to choose wisely: a bed loses its resale value even faster than a Honda. But we looked at so many beds I suspect we became confused about what we were buying. A park, perhaps? A picnic spot, a sports arena, a conference centre? In other words, a status symbol. The bed we finally chose said, in Sleepcity talk, *You have arrived.*

We had taken out an option on nocturnal separation. You said in a silly voice that we were embracing change and personal growth. I thought, more like we were asking for trouble. In a bed that size intimacy is not inevitable. It must be initiated and, remembering back to the days of manually changing TV channels, I was all too aware of how easily effort can outweigh desire.

But no. From the start, by unspoken agreement, we established a ritual of touch. My foot your foot your hand my neck my belly your back my knee your thigh my thigh your bum. There you are. Connection. Contentment.

Yesterday I had lunch with Rebecca — please bear with me: this is not a *non sequitur*. We went to a Turkish café I'd never even noticed before. A narrow dark room tucked in behind New Regent Street. Incense and backpackers and brandy-strength coffee — all the things Rebecca misses. Back three weeks and already she's homesick for the rest of the world.

She'd finally used up her last film and had it developed. So I'm sorry, but you've missed out on Tibet. It's her favourite country. I hadn't realised, but this was her third visit there since the break-up with Tony.

A background of mountains in virtually every shot. She spent five weeks trekking down valleys and up mountain passes, smiling at sherpas and practising basic German and French on fellow travellers. She's so scornful of 'tourists' — those who gawp through glass as they journey in air-conditioned comfort from one standardised hotel to another. Yet I suspect the locals prefer those types. Well, wouldn't you? Given the choice between package tourists who spend lots of money and stick with their own kind, and convoys of over-loaded snails trudging right past your door?

There were photos of streams and rocky terrain, of monks and temples and women burdened by heavy loads. (Not all of them backpackers.) It was like thumbing through a copy of National Geographic.

Rebecca would point to people in parkas, dreadlocks, polar fleece jackets and give them a name and a potted CV. Harry, the medical student from Amsterdam, was in a number of photos, looking morose. His girlfriend, said Rebecca, had swapped him in Barcelona for a well-built data analyst from Ghana.

I pretended envy, as one feels obliged to do. (Of Rebecca, that is, not Harry's ex-girlfriend.) And there was a time when travel was on my agenda. I had a desire back then to be non-accountable; I could see myself as a sponge soaking up exotic sensations and, possibly, knowledge. Also I'd noticed that people with accents got more attention.

That time has long gone. Though Rebecca believed in my envy, in fact seemed to take it for granted. These days there's a layer of incomprehension between the two of us. I still belong to the time of Rebecca and Tony, whereas she has moved on. I suspect she pities me. Over lunch I saw her frustration at being unable to convey properly the pleasure of walking in sturdy shoes in a continent where there is no one you've known for longer than a week, and with no certain knowledge as to where you will sleep that night, or the next, or the one after that. (That part I could, I felt, understand or at least imagine: the soaring freedom of unpredictability.)

But she wanted more from me than the ability to imagine; she wanted my conversion. Just as I, in turn, wanted hers.

I wanted to tell her about our feet stretching across that private cricket field to meet and entwine. That (I wanted to say) is another

9

kind of journey and not — as she well knew — exactly predictable. Especially in a bed the size of a ballroom.

In Madrid (she sent us that postcard, remember?) Rebecca met up with Alicia as they had planned. I would have liked to see Alicia — she's twenty-three already — but that film was in the camera that got stolen in Morocco.

Alicia now has a Celtic tattoo and an unseen lover. She pours out her heart and mind in Internet cafés. ' Steamy and safe,' said Rebecca approvingly. The lover lives in Colorado and the two have agreed never to meet. Theirs is a spiritual/cerebral passion. The lover has compared it to a bottle of vintage wine: once opened it can only be emptied or else lose its flavour.

Rebecca relayed this wisdom in tones of respect.

I thought of Alicia the last time we saw her. She was maybe fifteen and had learnt to read Tarot cards. She sat on our carpet and interpreted my life, though diplomatically, as unthreatened and unremarkable. Now I feel sad on her account. Partly because of the cyber lover, but mostly because of Rebecca's glowing approval.

Do you think I should sit Rebecca down, perhaps on the edge of our bed, and talk to her about options and journeys? But what would I say?

Maybe if I, too, had photos to show? My foot your foot your hand my neck my belly your back.

My sole, your sole.

LIFE ON EARTH

The dress is pale blue taffeta with silly little pintucks beneath a peter pan collar. It's stiff and shiny and when she moves the flared skirt catches against itself and hisses. And the cap sleeves stick out like sharp little wings. If she had a wand and was four years old . . .

Audrey is familiar with all these details — taffeta, pintucks, peter pan collar — only because her mother referred to them constantly, glancing up from her new electric Singer that does buttonholes and zigzag and overlocking. The dress required numerous tryings-on; Audrey in her embarrassing bra and her saggy bloomers standing solid and goosebumped in the cold sunporch while her mother transferred pins from mouth to seams and tucks and pleats. Audrey watching all the while in case someone should circle their drive and see her through the window, lumpy and white or draped in hostile fabric.

The dress is proof of Audrey's mother's dislike. Or at least her

11

permanent disappointment. Though, to be fair, on the cover of the Butterick pattern it did not look at all the way it looks on Audrey. In the Butterick sketch the woman seems to have tripped — her arms are flung out and her long, perfect legs are ungrounded. Both her hair and the dress have been caught in graceful motion. Even so, Audrey wasn't impressed. The dress looked, she had sullenly muttered, like something you'd put on a toddler.

'You have to cater for figure types,' said her mother. 'It's no good stuffing yourself into a dress that will do your shape no favours at all.'

Audrey's shape is not unlike a toddler's. Except, that is, for her bust, which is, in her boarding school dormitory, an object of awe and mild hysteria. The pintucks are there to divert the eye away from that bosom. Audrey's mother is an expert on the tricks and rules of fashion.

In the mirror Audrey stares with dismay at her taffeta self, so stiff and palely blue. Her head and neck appear to be balanced on the peter pan collar in the manner of a severed royal head on a velvet cushion. Audrey would not be surprised if blood began to seep into the pintucked front. The dress is mid-calf because this is in fashion.

Audrey tilts the mirror to look at mid-calf and the strappy black evening sandals, flat because of her height. 'You won't get boys by towering over them,' her mother had said, so Audrey had agreed to the flat sandals, though she tried on heels anyway and they definitely made her legs look better. If she leans forward she can see the toes, ugly with reinforced nylon. Audrey's legs are brown from the sun but her mother says no one would dream of going dancing in bare legs and Audrey definitely doesn't want to stand out as different. Having to go to this dance is misery enough.

'I'd rather not,' she'd said from the start, but her mother predicted she'd change her mind so the dress was made. And now, after 'all that effort', Audrey's mother requires the dress to be worn.

Audrey's mother has made arrangements for Audrey to be driven to the dance by Andrew Bassett, who is seventeen and has his driver's licence. Andrew's mother and Audrey's mother are friends. Twice a week they share a car into town to play bridge with a bunch of other women.

Andrew will be also taking his cousin, Pamela. Audrey's mother admires both Andrew and Pamela. 'They have such lovely manners. They both speak up so nicely when spoken to. They never mumble. They have sensible things to say for themselves. And they're such attractive young people, always so nicely turned out.'

Audrey's mother has a story she likes to tell about Andrew handing out scones at afternoon tea. 'The last for the best,' he had said to Audrey's mother. She's never forgotten. 'I'll never forget . . .' she says whenever the Bassetts are mentioned, then goes on to tell the story once again. And at the end she always says, 'Such a charmer, even at that age. Just like his father, I seem to remember.' And she gives a secret smile as if there is another, more interesting, story that she might, if pressed, be willing to divulge.

Audrey's hair is determined to curl, even though she waited until it was dry before removing the scarf she'd bound about her head like a bandage. Curly hair is not in fashion: even Audrey knows this.

On her mother's advice Audrey has smeared her lips with Tangy Natural. 'Just a little or you'll have yourself looking like some cheap tart.' Audrey wishes this was even remotely possible. She leans in close to the bathroom mirror to find out how she might look in the eyes of someone about to kiss her. She sees her eyelashes, pale and stubby, and her freckles like so many dandelions. She sees her lips, puckered and orange-tinted, and her neck in the peter pan collar.

Perhaps the kiss could happen outside in the dark.

At Audrey's age her mother had so many boy 'admirers' it was hard to choose.

Audrey is relieved to see that Andrew is now taller than she is.

'I knew you wouldn't be one of those rude young fellows who sit in the car and toot,' simpers Audrey's mother.

Audrey's father shakes Andrew's hand. 'I'd offer you a drink, lad, but you're driving.'

'Thanks, Mr Nelson,' says Andrew, as if the drink is on offer anyway, 'but Pamela's waiting in the car.'

'Right, mustn't keep the ladies waiting. It's okay for them, but not for us.'

Audrey's father has made a joke, so they all laugh.

'Keep an eye on her, Andrew, there's a good fellow,' he now says. 'It's her first dance.'

Audrey wants to hide or die.

'Put on your stole, Audrey,' says her mother. 'It's chilly out there.'

The stole was a gift from Audrey's Aunty Pat. It is mohair and looks and feels like a white Persian cat curled around Audrey's shoulders.

'Love your stole,' says Pamela as Audrey folds herself into the back seat of Mr Bassett's new black Vauxhall.

'Have a nice time,' calls her mother, and for a second or two Audrey thinks maybe she will; maybe having a nice time is not entirely out of the question.

Audrey did not know a night could go on for so long.

At first she sticks with Pamela, whose dress is softly green with shoelace straps, and whose hair is pale and straight, caught back by an alice band the exact colour of her dress. Audrey and Pamela went to the same small primary school. Pamela was two years ahead of Audrey but they sat in the same classroom because that's all there was — one classroom, a very small kitchen and the concrete porch.

When they picked teams for tip-and-he-runs Pamela had twice

chosen Audrey, even though she was no good at catching or throwing and even worse at batting. Usually Audrey would have to stand there until everyone, even the littlest kids, had been picked. And then, if the teams were even, the teacher would add her to the best team as a handicap.

Audrey still feels grateful to Pamela for that kindness.

Although there is no one here from Audrey's class there is a handful of kids she knows from primary school. She says hello to them but is not disappointed when they don't stop to talk. They did not pick her for tip-and-he-runs and anyway, even two years seems a long time ago; what would they talk about? Audrey already knows who are class captains and who are prefects and who is getting herself a bad reputation. She even knows what they plan to do on leaving school. Her mother has told her. Audrey's mother and her friends depend on other people's lives for things to talk about.

At first the band just messes about making noises while everyone stands around the sides of the hall and a couple of fathers shake white powder onto the floor. Audrey keeps her stole around her neck, hiding the peter pan collar, and Pamela stands beside her making polite conversation in the bright, high voice that so impresses Audrey's mother.

But then it's the First Waltz and Pamela is taken away by a dark-haired boy. Audrey is left on the girls' side of the hall, gradually edging closer and closer to the wall, with its forms for sitting on, as the seated girls get picked away. When the music ends Pamela doesn't come back to stand with Audrey. The next dance, a foxtrot, most of the girls get asked and the dancing couples take up so much space that Audrey is obliged to sit on the wooden form with the other three who are left. They perch there side by side like sparrows on a power line and it's tip-and-he-runs all over again, only much, much worse.

Audrey concentrates on things. On the high windows above the door, on the red and blue streamers that twist and droop from the centre of the ceiling to the wooden picture rail that Audrey could easily reach by standing on the form should she feel inclined to tug them down. On her own hands with the clear nail varnish, which was all she was allowed and which, given the state of her nails, was hardly worth the effort.

She barely glances at those on the dance floor in case that may be construed as envy. And now and again she smiles, as if at some happy private thought, for the benefit of whoever might be watching.

She allows herself to imagine who this watcher might be. Stuart Allardice. Who is here in a light brown suit with a jacket so loose it flaps from his shoulders, and no sign of a tie. Stuart Allardice, who lived in town (his father still owns the fish and chip shop) but used to ride out on his motorbike and work for the farmers in his varsity holiday, and now has a job in the city with the Public Trust. Which explains why he is here because this dance is not open to riff-raff. Audrey would not be allowed to attend the kind that is. This dance is for the boys and girls who are home from boarding school, plus a few selected extras to make up the numbers.

She chooses Stuart Allardice for the story she will tell Jackie and Lynn when term begins. How he danced with her three times (no point in making it unbelievable) and then took her outside to kiss her and put a hand down her dress. (Jackie will want to know more; Lynn will squeal.) He gave her his address and asked her to write to him, but she may not bother.

Andrew asks her for the third dance. A quickstep. Audrey reads in his face that he is reluctantly obeying his mother's orders. Knowing that feeling only too well, she does her best to make conversation, even though she is already over-familiar with the subject of Andrew Bassett.

He plans to be an accountant and make lots of money, and then take over the farm. The meals at his school are lousy, but Andrew and his friends get up to all sorts of 'larks'. Audrey has never heard that word used in this way, though she has come across it in books. When she gets back to school she'll try it out on Jackie and Lynn. It can be their new word for next term. 'What a lark,' they'll say to each other and roll about clutching their bellies.

When the dance ends Andrew briskly deposits Audrey back among the unwanted girls. He has not set a trend; no other young men follow in his wake. The band labours steadily through the programme pinned on the wall. Veleta, foxtrot, gay gordons . . .

The band is four old men. Audrey recognises one of them as the father of Leon Hargreaves, who once had a fit on the school porch and she knew she should find his tongue but his head was thrashing about. Leon is here, wearing his hair slicked back, all black and shiny to match his shoes.

At school there is dancing class between dinner and prep every second Tuesday. Step slide-slide step slide-slide turn. Audrey always has to be the man because of her size. Other nights, in the gym, they rock 'n' roll to Bill Hayley and Elvis and Little Richard. Audrey can swing her friends through her legs from behind without losing the beat. She can flip them right up and over her back to land feet first.

Lynn gets to go to those kinds of dances, or says she does. She wears flat shoes and a belt cinched so tight she can hardly breathe and young men in drape coats toss her over their shoulders, then take her outside and try to remove her bloomers.

There are twenty dances listed tonight, not one of them rock 'n' roll.

Not wanting to sit with the unpartnered girls Audrey finds things to do. She visits the toilet and on her way back detours to the kitchen, where mothers are making club sandwiches, slicing up fruit and heating sausage rolls. There is a debate underway about how long it takes for sliced banana to discolour and whether or not lemon juice makes much difference. When she is noticed Audrey offers to help. 'No, no,' they tell her. 'This is your night, get back in there and enjoy yourself.'

Leon Hargreaves has danced three times with Pamela. 'Oh, not again,' she says and ducks behind Audrey, who wouldn't say no. The next dance is the Supper Waltz and she worries that those who don't get to dance may not get to eat. In the kitchen she'd sighted pavlovas awaiting cream, their exposed sides as pale and tender as her inner arm. She hopes they will not be ruined by chinese gooseberries just for the sake of a splash of colour.

'Hello, Leon,' says Audrey.

'Audrey,' says Leon, 'have you seen Pamela?'

The band is into the second chorus of *The Tennessee Waltz* but Audrey can't bring herself to sit once again alongside the other undanced-with darlings. She edges herself, a few steps at a time, towards the door.

Outside a group of young men in stovepipe trousers and high slicked bodgie hair are loafing in front of the hall, and a couple who ought to be waltzing are giggling and kissing in the shadows beside the fence. Up above there are stars, struggling against the glow of the streetlight.

'Hey, you,' calls one of the bodgies.

Audrey looks behind her.

'No, you. Baby doll.'

His friends laugh.

'Sexy dress,' says one of them, and Audrey grins. She knows she should be offended but they remind her of Lynn and Jackie.

The one who spoke first holds up a bottle. ' I s'pose you'd be too stuck up to drink with us.'

The bottle is only half full and in the street light the empty amber glass has a jewel-like glow. Audrey smiles. She would like to go over and join them. They are the friendliest anyone has been to her all evening. But the Supper Waltz couple are watching; they have heard the exchange, and if she accepts it will simply confirm her contemptibility.

Audrey re-enters the hall. In her brief absence the leftover girls have dwindled. If Audrey had stayed she might be up there with the lucky ones, blushing and stumbling. Or have they just fled to the washroom?

Audrey looks at the two who are left. One has a cleft palate, her top lip hooked up like a dropped stitch, and the other wears glasses with lenses so thick her eyes seem to press up against them. Their dresses are both much nicer than Audrey's. They sit on the form with a big space between them. Audrey sits down in the middle and the one with the glasses edges aside a little as if to make room.

This is worse — much, much worse — than tip-and-he-runs. Into Audrey's head come a string of lambs trotting along the narrow race in her father's yards. Audrey is at the dividing gate, channelling them into one pen or the other depending on the colour of the raddle streak her father has swiped on their backs. Red for the good ones, blue for the runts. Audrey reflects on the grim fate of those that are chosen.

Even so, she wants to be one of them.

She tries to talk to the cleft palate girl. *Where do you live? What school do you go to?* The replies, perhaps because the music is loud, are indecipherable. Audrey nods and smiles.

A couple of fathers have appeared from nowhere and are waiting with trestles and table tops for the dance floor to clear. Behind them hover the mothers with loaded plates and bowls. The band stops playing before the song is ready to end and at once there is a confusion of people coming and going. Some of the boys lend a hand with the tables. Audrey takes note of cold chicken, sausage rolls and savoury eggs before her view is blocked by hovering couples.

The cleft palate girl touches Audrey's arm. 'We're allowed to eat?' she worries, and this time Audrey has no trouble understanding.

'We must be.' She jumps up and bends over the girl in glasses. 'Let's get in quick before it's all gone.'

They edge and shuffle their way to the table and load their plates with more than they want. They stand in a tight little scrum with their backs to everyone. The one in the glasses is happy to take Audrey's three slices of chinese gooseberry.

Too soon the parents are clearing away the tables and the musicians are mooching back wiping froth from their lips. Audrey follows her supper friends back to their lonely seat. As the band starts up the girl with the glasses leans towards her ear.

'You're lucky,' she says in loud whisper. 'At least you had one dance.'

This time it's a quickstep, and Stuart Allardice is with a girl with her hair piled up, the way they're all wearing it in the latest issue of *McCall's*. And there's Pamela . . . Mrs Curtis would have a fit. A hand must at all times easily slide between dancing pairs. A theoretical hand, that is, or Mrs Curtis's, by way of demonstration. Not a hand belonging to either of the dancers concerned.

Audrey wants to go home but Pamela is clinging to some big-eared boy and Andrew is nowhere to be seen.

Audrey stands up. 'I might just have lost my lift home,' she tells her companions. Vacating her place beside them feels like desertion. She edges her way to the door a few steps at a time so as not to seem eager.

The bodgies have gone and it's cold without her stole, which, on her last visit, she left in the washroom on a pile of stoles and fluffy jackets. She can't go back and get it. On the footpath she turns right towards the town, walking briskly to keep warm. She walks past the closed-up shops, then turns right again and walks past the houses, looking in through all the lit windows. Little blasts of music come out to greet her. Buddy Holly and the Platters. Inside the windows mothers tidy their kitchens and men play cards.

In the next street it's harder to see because of the trees. Not much music here, but sometimes the plum-in-the-mouth voices of the National Programme. Audrey's mother admires stuck-up. The people all seem to be reading or knitting. No one out on the footpath but Audrey and the occasional cat. Again Audrey looks up at the stars. Apart from the glittering Evening Star she only knows them as congregations: the Milky Way, the Iron Pot. Up there among them, hurtling through black space, is Sputnik 2, a capsule containing a terrified dog.

Or maybe not. Jackie says not. Her father was someone important during the war and knows such things. He says it's just communist propaganda. There was no Sputnik 1, and there is no Sputnik 2, no astro-dog. What people are seeing is shooting stars. The human race is easily fooled.

Audrey, Lynn and Jackie used to sit on the fire escape sharing a blanket until almost three in the morning, but there was nothing to see except stars and the edge of the moon. They wished on the stars, then forced each other to tell what they'd wished for. Audrey wished for a different mother.

Heading back to the hall she can pick out the military two-step. (There's a name that has all three of them splitting their sides.) Around the block again, this time in a marching-skipping gait until the beat is lost in a blur of sound. Then Audrey slows down into a kind of shuffle that Lynn describes as jive. She imagines Sammy Davis Junior's shiny pointed shoes tapping along beside her shiny strappy ones.

Back at the hall and it's a waltz and maybe, with luck, the last. The wooden form is unoccupied. The girl with glasses is dancing with a boy who only comes up to her chin and the cleft palate girl is nowhere to be seen. Audrey edges her way to the kitchen where the mothers and one father are doing the dishes. She picks up a damp teatowel and helps.

'Thank you, dear.' The mother beside her exchanges the damp towel for a dry one. 'Are you all right?'

'Yes,' says Audrey.

'Almost finished,' says the mother cheerfully, but Audrey fears she's only talking about the dishes.

This time it really is the Last Waltz: she heard it announced. There's nothing left to do in the kitchen so Audrey makes her way to the washroom to collect her stole, and all but collides with Euan Sanders, who was a year behind her and good at woodwork.

'Audrey,' he says, 'do you know how to dance? I'm not very good.'

And he isn't. They stumble around looking down at his feet with Audrey advising, but she's not used to being the girl and that's hard enough. Then it's over: it's finally over and time to go home. She collects her stole and almost runs to the car. Andrew's voice is both slower and louder than it was before. He holds a back door open for Audrey and the front one for Pamela. 'You girls enjoy yourselves?'

'Yes, thank you,' says Audrey.

'You know Christine Levison?' says Pamela. 'How they said she'd gone to Noumea with her French class? Well, actually she's up the duff.'

Audrey doesn't know Christine Levison. She lets her body fall sideways along the seat, which smells new and shiny. She bundles the stole up into a pillow and closes her eyes. She concentrates on right turns and left turns and gear changes. This is how it would be if she was kidnapped, trussed up and tossed in the boot of the car: she would chart the journey by movement and sound.

Once they have turned off the main road the tyres scrunch now and again into loose metal and Pamela shrieks, 'Andy!' and Andrew says, 'Whoops.'

And now they slow down and pull over as if to stop, though they can't be much more than halfway, not even past the quarry.

And they have stopped, but Audrey keeps her eyes closed: she doesn't know why.

'She still asleep?' It's barely a whisper.

Audrey can feel Pamela's eyes sliding over her. 'Like a baby.'

'Good.' A creak of upholstery. 'My lucky night.'

Pamela giggles faintly and after that there is no more talking, just rabbity scuffling sounds and, occasionally, a moist, slurping, squelch of mouth or tongue. These go on for a very long time. Someone is breathing hard in the way of an agitated bull, so it's surely Andrew. And those small squeaks are Pamela. Audrey's eyes are still shut; to open them now would be like cheating. She attempts, without moving, to block her ears. She should not be here. She does not want to see or hear; she wants to cry. This is even worse than sitting, unchosen, on the wooden form.

How long will they be? Audrey's leg is numb. She turns in a sleeping kind of way so her back is towards them.

They're cousins. At this thought Audrey opens her eyes. Out the car's back window the stars are bright, and there's one that's moving. A small shining pinprick of light sliding across the pitch-black sky. Sputnik 2? There were hazy newspaper photos of the dog, a black and white terrier-cross by name of Laila. Trapped, like it or not, in a metal capsule for reasons beyond her comprehension.

It's okay, girl, Audrey transmits. At least you're not wearing a peter pan collar.

She decides she'll tell the truth to Lynn and Jackie: it's awful enough to please them greatly. She imagines the three of them help-lessly gasping and writhing, and hastily stuffs her mouth with mohair in case her own laughter erupts in advance. In the front seats things have gone very quiet.

The motor starts and as they move off Pamela thumps around uncrumpling herself.

'Hey,' says Audrey in a thickened voice, raising her head.

23

'Where are we? What's happened?'

'Not far now,' says Andrew. 'You've been asleep.'

'So you had a good time?' Her father is buttering toast.

'Okay,' she mumbles.

'Pardon?' says her mother.

'Yes,' Audrey enunciates, 'it was all right.'

'There. What did I tell you? And Andrew danced with you?'

'Yes.'

'Well, of course. He has such lovely manners. And Pamela too. They both speak up so clearly and nicely.'

Audrey swallows scrambled eggs. She's careful not to let her fork scrape against the plate. A gust of rain spatters the kitchen windows.

Audrey's mother sets her knife and fork down side by side. She dabs at her mouth with her napkin. 'That reminds me,' she says in a tinkling voice, 'of a time when Eva had invited me around for afternoon tea. And Andrew — he was only a youngster then, but already he had his father's charm . . .'

CASTER SUGAR

'Caster sugar,' she says again. Her fingers, pale and thin and weighted with rings, drum on the counter.

'Caster sugar. Yes.' He heard the first time. He's seeing castors, slightly rusted. Some kind of oil?

'I've searched the shelves.' Her voice has risen. She is distressed. Her need for this caster sugar is urgent.

'Then we have none,' says Al. 'No caster sugar.'

'None at all?'

'None at all.' He's aware of another customer, a man with yellow tinted shades, streaked hair and a tunnel of earrings in his visible ear. He's taking an interest in this exchange from the neutral territory of the magazine stand.

Those who browse, or pretend to browse, are not to be trusted. Dennis, on Al's first day. *And if some bugger's keeping an eye on you that's reason to keep two eyes on him. Or her. We all fall into the trap*

25

of imagining that tits make them more honest.

'I don't think I've ever had that thought exactly,' Al told Dennis. But he's noticed, since then, that it's the men he instinctively looks for in the angled mirror.

Now he has a good reason not to go out the back and search for caster (Car-Star? Kahsta?) sugar.

'This is unbelievable,' says the woman. Laying such stress on the word that Al imagines her raising two sets of hooked fingers — quote, unquote. 'And you call this a shop!' she fires over her shoulder as she marches out into the sunlight.

The man at the magazine stand throws Al a grin. Perhaps Al himself was already smirking. The woman had meant to upset him by insulting the place. As if it was his shop, as if he *cared*, as if he wanted to be here with all these foodstuffs and products he'd never heard of until three weeks ago. Bioluvil, Demarara, Napisan, Nutribites . . . a whole language he'd never learnt. A language that, unbeknown to him, Sylvie knew and spoke every day.

That's the thing that startles him, even now — that she had these spheres of capability he'd simply never given thought to. She had been a raft on which, for thirty-five years, he had floated comfortably over the deep holes and perplexing rapids of daily survival. Now that she's gone he's in there floundering and sliding on boulders. How will he manage when it comes to the deep dark pools?

Al has another customer, one of the locals who knew Sylvie. Perhaps they worked together? She'd talked to Al after the funeral. He remembers this clearly because the woman had looked like someone Sylvie would get along with. In fact she'd looked a bit like Sylvie. Cheerful, capable, middle-aged; the kind of woman who would not, could not, suddenly die and let everyone down.

'So how is it?' Her eyes do a kindly search of Al's as she sets a handful of goods on the counter. Tea bags, yoghurt, eggs and a packet of freezer bags; nothing unfamiliar there.

'Not bad,' he mumbles. 'Yeah, okay.' His standard reply to questions on how he is managing. The right reply, for he senses their relief. To them he is just the husband of that nice woman who worked at the library. They do not want to be burdened with his loneliness. Al slides the scanner over barcodes.

'This must be a bit of a shock for the system.' Her look takes in the three small aisles and the man at the magazine stand. 'But I guess it fills in the time.'

'Yes,' says Al, 'it does that.' He packs the items into a plastic bag, eggs on top. He feels the woman's sympathy, her kindly concern, like soup simmering on a cold day. Like Sylvie. He's aware that the exchange must seem one-sided and makes an effort. 'I seem to be getting the hang of it,' he offers. Then adds, by way of insurance because they all know one another here, 'It was good of Dennis to take me on.'

The man has left the magazine rack and is hovering near the fruit and veges. Al sees him in the mirror pick up an orange and stare at it.

'Well, I hope he's paying you what you're worth.'

Al grins. 'I couldn't get by if he did.'

The man has turned his back on the fruit. Al can't blame him; it sits there so long he has to wipe off the dust.

If you don't stock it, they want it, says Dennis. *Rule of thumb. And when you do stock it they tell you they can get it cheaper and fresher at the supermarket. We're the hidden component of the road toll statistics. The cheap Jap imports are killing us off.*

'Take care,' says the woman, sliding the plastic bag from the counter.

'Caster sugar,' says Al quickly. 'What is it?'

'Just sugar, ground up fine.'

'Ah,' he says. 'Thank you.'

His ignorance has pleased her. Her smile is still there as she turns into the street.

The man in the yellow glasses finally speaks. 'You use it to make pavlovas,' he offers from the breakfast food section. And Al remembers tilting a cup slowly so the contents trickled like fine white sand into the clouds of egg white while Sylvie wielded the beater. Long ago, before he became the father who put on a suit and drove each day to the city.

The man has removed his glasses and is looking at Al. He has astonishing eyes — deep sea green made tender by long black lashes. Al knows those eyes; he has seen them before, and close up. Perhaps in a magazine?

'You're Al Slater.' It's not exactly a question. Narrow, eager lips with a nervous twitch. Familiar yet unplaceable.

'Remember me?'

Al opens his mouth, as if a name is on its way.

'Osmond.'

'Osmond. Of course. Good God, Oz.' Al narrows his eyes, the better to locate the adolescent beneath those settled features, and Osmond, smiling, steps forward to shake hands.

'I thought you might not . . .'

'Of course we would. Our favourite babysitter.'

'How are they? Jo and Max?'

As if it were only a couple of years.

'Fine. Yeah, good. Jo's got a couple of young ones. Actually they were up here just . . .' Al trails off. Does Osmond know? Is that why he's here? 'You just . . . sort of . . . passing through?'

'No,' says Osmond. 'Well, sort of.' He shuffles a bit, looks at the sign that says, Sorry, we don't give credit. 'I went to look for our old place. Should'a guessed.'

'That's how it goes,' says Al. 'Whole outfit has gone upmarket.'

'Tell me about it,' says Osmond darkly. 'Shops 'n' all.' He brightens a little. 'You guys' place looks much the same.'

'It shouldn't. We've ploughed in a small fortune, but it's all out the back. Extensions, proper verandah, the works.'

To enjoy, they'd said, in their old age.

The way she would touch him as she passed, or suddenly take his hand in hers. His flesh now shrivelling from lack of a habit so ingrained he'd ceased to notice.

'Mean-looking redhead,' says Osmond, 'in our place. Where it was. She said I'd find you here.'

'Mrs Kalman.' Next door but one. Sylvie would know her first name.

'What else did she tell you?' Hoping she might have done it for him, this woman he barely knows.

Osmond stares at Al for a moment, then grins. 'You two been busted or something?'

Al shakes his head. He should be amused — and not just for the benefit of the young woman at the chiller who is bound to be listening. The idea is so far off track, so locked in a distant past. But that 'you two' has ripped across his heart like a thorny twig.

The woman, who has cruelly sunburnt shoulders, steps up behind Osmond with a look that says she is angry already at the prospect of waiting while these two chat. But Osmond gives her his faltering smile and steps aside. She is placated. A packet of toilet rolls and a carton of cream: a holidaymaker's purchase. While Al drops them into a bag a carload of youngsters push in through the door — loud voices and helpless laughter. Al rolls his eyes at Osmond by way of apology.

'I could come back.' There's a pleading note in the younger man's voice.

'If you're not in hurry, yeah, do.' Al is trying to keep his two eyes on all five youngsters. 'I finish at six, we could have a drink. I could maybe even knock up a meal.'

Now Osmond reads between the lines. 'You and Sylvie . . .' His face, Al sees, has gone tight with dismay, or even anger.

'Ah,' stalls Al, eyes back on the job. It's seven weeks, for Chrissake, there must be a right way of saying this and he should know it by now.

'I'll be at your place just after six.' Osmond heads off abruptly, one hand in the air, perhaps waving, perhaps to shut out whatever it is that Al might be about to say.

Back then it was just a beach at the end of a winding, unsealed road. A scattered collection of holiday baches, no store, no service station. Al and Sylvie fled here, escaping the irrelevancy of tutorials and assignments. Passion had obscured their uncertain visions of unspecified careers. Besides, Sylvie was pregnant.

Al got casual work on the surrounding farms — farmers were still making a decent living — and battled to save his dope plants from determined opossums. Sylvie baked bread, tended an ever-extending garden and listened to the National Programme. They had a daughter, then a son.

One by one the beach baches became permanent homes for people escaping from one thing or another. Bronwyn and Charlie, Osmond's mother and stepfather, rented the Tickners' bach. They'd fled from the King's Cross drug scene, though for a time they kept this information to themselves.

On his own Charlie might have stuck it out. But Charlie was fond of Osmond and besotted with Bron, and Bron needed excitement, complexity. One way or another she was born to score.

Bron's eyes. Sea green, black fringed, just like Osmond's except there was more going on inside them.

You couldn't trust Bron. Sylvie said so right from the start. Women like her, said Sylvie, had no scruples. But Al and Charlie became good mates, so Sylvie and Bron saw a lot of each other and became friends of a kind.

'She's after you,' Sylvie told Al, and he'd laughed at the bristling tone of her voice.

'Don't look so smug,' Sylvie snapped. 'It's not a compliment. It's not even to do with you — it's about her and me.'

Al was still grinning. 'A competition? And I'm the prize!'

The briefest of smiles as she shook her head. 'The prize is . . . winning.'

'But Bron really likes you,' Al said, bemused. 'You know she does.'

Sylvie flapped her hands about as if, that way, they might happen upon the words she was seeking. 'It's not *personal*,' she said. 'It's bigger than personal. It's about *things*.'

'Things?'

'Like what we believe in.'

'You think Bron needs you to be like her?'

'*No.*' She was impatient with his refusal to see. 'Just, her and me, the way we see things . . . One of us has to be wrong.' She scanned Al's face for comprehension, then shook her head. 'Forget it,' she said. 'Forget it.'

Over coffee or gins Bron would tell Sylvie about things she'd done or watched being done. Sexual acts. Which, later and in private, Sylvie would relate to Al. As, Al guessed with a tweak of excitement, Bron had intended her to.

Osmond was fifteen or thereabouts — a shy and startlingly beautiful boy. His father, according to Bron, had been a Portuguese sailor. Oz spent so much time at Al and Sylvie's they ceased to be aware of his presence. He was good at blending in.

When Sylvie and Al and Charlie and Bron trekked off to the city to see Bob Marley at Western Springs, or were invited to one of the increasingly numerous local parties, Osmond would mind the

31

children. In hindsight this makes Al feel uneasy, but back then trust came more readily. Besides, the children were very fond of Oz.

Right from the start Bron spent a good deal of time in the city. With her sister, she said, and Charlie seemed to believe this even if Sylvie didn't. One day while Bron was away the drug squad arrived and removed the three malnourished plants that Bronwyn had shoved among the straggling geraniums beside their toolshed. They also took Charlie, who had prior convictions. Oz was there. He didn't come to Sylvie and Al's but stayed in the house alone until Sylvie, having heard that Charlie had been seen in the back of a cop car, went over and fetched him.

A couple of mornings later Bron's car was parked in the driveway. Oz didn't look eager to go across so Sylvie went with him. She followed him in the open front door and saw him stop mid-stride. Then he turned and steered Sylvie out of the house.

'Bron's sleeping,' he told her. 'I'll come back later.'

But Sylvie had seen what Osmond had seen — Bron like a vacuum cleaner at a groin attached to a pair of muscular legs. Her eyes were on her son, her head still in motion.

'Perhaps,' said Al weakly, 'she thought the situation was beyond retrieving.'

Bronwyn's new partner was Kerran, who came from Kaikoura but looked like a Californian beach bum. He was five years older than Osmond.

'My two gorgeous darlings,' gushed Bron the first time Al and Sylvie came over. 'My dark boy and my golden boy. Aren't they both so very delicious?' She patted and stroked the pair of them, her eyes on Al. Kerran laughed and nipped at her hand with his gleaming teeth while Oz's face was a faintly smiling mask. And she laughed to fill the silence that followed.

On the subject of Charlie, all Bron had to say was that cops had always been bastards and always would be.

Now Oz only called at Sylvie and Al's in the company of Kerran, or Kerran and Bron. And that wasn't often; for Charlie's sake Al and Sylvie were less than hospitable. But Al would see Oz and Kerran down the beach: the golden one setting the pace, brushing his long hair out of his eyes, the dark one behind him, a shadow with a surfboard.

Sylvie worried about the boy. 'See his eyes,' she fretted. 'Like glass. You can't get in there any more.'

'Stoned,' guessed Al.

'Who could blame him?'

She waited for a response but Al said nothing. *Whatever you're thinking, don't say it or we'll start believing it. And anyway it's none of our business.*

'Stoned is bad enough,' said Sylvie. 'He's just a kid.'

'But not our kid,' said Al. Too fast, too firmly, for Sylvie gave him one of her looks.

Charlie was remanded in custody for a week, then sentenced to six months on account of having a record. Al would have made the trip to court if Bron or Osmond had let him know. Charlie served four months in a minimum-security jail a five-hour drive away. Bron and Oz went down twice to visit, and Al went once on his own. Charlie seemed happy enough. He made no mention of Kerran, so neither did Al, though Sylvie insisted that Charlie had a right to know.

'He may not want to know,' Al offered on his return. 'I suspect I wouldn't, in his position.'

'I'm not thinking of Charlie,' said Sylvie. 'He needs to know for Oz's sake. Someone needs to step in or what kind of a man is that poor kid going to grow into?'

By the time Charlie got out Kerran had left. Charlie hitch-hiked home. He claimed there was a mix-up over his release date, but maybe he'd thought to catch Bron out. That night the three of them

33

came to visit, just as they used to. Charlie told a few jail stories, but other than that it was as if the last few months had never happened.

Then within a week they'd gone. No warning, no goodbye, just one day the house was empty and a couple of days later Kath Tickner called in to ask Sylvie if they'd left a forwarding address — there was the matter of unpaid rent.

Al walks up the road with a carton of beer and two packets of frozen gourmet meals. Osmond is waiting outside the gate in a yellow car, a gleaming two-seater sports. Either a rental or Osmond is doing well for himself, Al thinks. He puts his hopes in the rental, since it seems unlikely that wealth would have come to Oz in legitimate ways.

'Nice car,' says Al as Oz climbs out clutching a bag from the local wine shop.

Oz looks pleased. Al sees, through the window, the Budget Rental tidy bag beneath the glovebox, but it only makes him feel sad.

'I brought some wine.' Osmond's voice trails off and up, turning it into a question.

'And I brought someone else's cooking.' Al raises the lightest of the plastic bags. 'I'm not too great in the kitchen.'

He leads the way through the gate. Best to get it said. 'Sylvie had a heart attack. Middle of February. It just . . . stopped, apparently. She was on her way home from work. You see that we've got a library now? Video shop. You name it. And we have to lock our doors.'

Al steps aside to let Oz enter. For a moment their eyes meet and Al has to remind himself that this is the son. 'They couldn't revive her,' he says. It's as if the words are on a record. Over and over. Round and round.

They walk through to the kitchen with its big rimu table and wide windows.

'It's like a different house,' says Oz, looking around. He puts the bottle on the bench. 'She was good, Sylvie,' he tells the ceiling.

'Yeah,' grunts Al. 'She was.'

He turns away to deal with desolation and to switch on the oven. Jo advised 180 degrees unless it said otherwise on the packet.

'I'd been retrenched,' he says, as if in explanation. 'Fifteen years and then laid off. Just a couple of months before . . .'

He wishes Oz would find something to say. And finally he does.

'So Joanne and Max, they're doing okay then?'

Gratefully Al gives him the details — location, jobs, partners, grandchild — while prising the caps off a couple of stubbies. He's aware that the information, as he presents it, is lean and colourless. He's unable to summon up those odd little incidents and asides that Sylvie would have added.

'Thanks.' Osmond accepts the bottle after a moment's hesitation. Does he not drink beer? Sylvie would have asked before the bottles were opened.

Osmond looks at Al and raises the bottle in a kind of salute.

'And Charlie?' Al asks, just a little tentatively, now that it's his turn. 'How's Charlie? And your mum?'

'Yeah, fine,' whispers Osmond, gazing out through the glass doors at Sylvie's flowers. His voice is so soft that Al has to repeat the words silently to himself.

Al clears a space on the table — the novel he can't get into, the *Listener*, unopened bills, a collection of glossy advertising leaflets, an invitation to take out life insurance. Oz, suddenly animated, has launched into a description of the house as it used to be, recalling details Al had long forgotten. Al has some difficulty concentrating on his words because suddenly it is Bron he's sitting across the table from. Her laugh, her elegant fingers, her greedy eyes grabbing at his like a hand on his balls.

Right from the start there were conversations he should have curtailed or reported to Sylvie. Though really they were nothing, a bit of fun. Sylvie didn't flirt; the point of it escaped her. Why bother, she'd say, unless you mean it?

Then without quite admitting it to himself, Al had begun to make an effort to be home when he thought Sylvie and the children would be out. Knowing that Bron was likely to drop in. A kid with the cookie jar, still just looking and wetting his lips. High on the dizzy mixture of longing and guilt, a sensation more intense than he'd ever imagined.

Osmond has run out of memories and vivacity. He closes one eye while the other looks bleakly down into the mouth of his half-full bottle. He hasn't yet explained what brought him back. A house that he lived in for less than three years, a bach that even then was due for demolition — that was not reason enough. It's not as though this beach is on the way to somewhere else, so that you might, on a whim, stop off.

But Al won't be pressing Osmond for a reason — the *real* reason. He doesn't have to. Inexplicably, but with certainty, Al now knows why Oz is here. He came looking for them, Al and Sylvie. But mostly Sylvie. Because . . . he could be sure of Sylvie. Was that it? Someone who didn't change, didn't pretend, didn't deceive. Sylvie as the mountain that would enable a grown-up Oz to find his bearings.

The back of Al's eyes ache at this thought of Oz in a landscape that may now be forever unfamiliar. He makes an effort.

'So when you guys left . . .' he prompts.

Oz seems to struggle back to the memory. 'Sydney, I think. Yeah, few days in Auckland, then back to Sydney.'

Al waits. Nothing.

'And that was okay?' he tries.

Oz shrugs. 'After a bit I shot through with a mate. Bundaberg. You know Bundaberg? Up north on the coast. Stayed there a while.'

Another silence. Al's eyes follow Oz's out to the garden. Finally he asks, 'And Kerran? You two stay in touch?'

What had she seen in him? Al had said just that, the day he went round there. Not long after he'd got back from seeing Charlie. Two hours of pretending things back at the beach were fine. What else can you do when a man's locked up?

He'd have it out with Bron. Make her see what she was doing.

Al waited for a big surf day when only he was home and Oz and Kerran had just gone by with their boards on Osmond's shoulder.

'So tell me. What's the attraction?'

Bron had laughed. Not in anger but delight.

'He knows what he wants.' She danced a few steps, turning her limbs at Egyptian angles. 'He's in tune with his hormones.'

'Unlike me?'

He'd reached for her then. Undone the knot that tied the sarong above her cleavage. Her bed — hers and Charlie's, hers and Kerran's — was unmade and smelt of sex and incense. He was aware of the need for haste: the boy must neither see nor guess.

She didn't climax, didn't even pretend for his sake. And, afterwards, when he searched her face for something that would explain or redeem, he saw only triumph, and remembered what Sylvie had said.

He wanted to swear Bron to secrecy but knew it was futile; she couldn't be trusted.

For a long time after he'd moved carefully, aware of his own breathing, like a man with a terminal illness. He noted what he had put in jeopardy and was appalled. Defensively he took to reading pulp magazine surveys on infidelity. Compared with most husbands he was almost a saint.

Yet he didn't — couldn't — tell Sylvie. Not even when Bron and Charlie had gone. He knew, by then, what Sylvie had known from the start. It was never about him; it was much bigger. Bigger even than Bron and Sylvie and what they believed in. It was fundamental and eternal. It was war, and Al was a traitor. A quisling.

He planned to tell Sylvie. Some day when the time was right. He knew this had to be done, for his secret was there between them like double glazing. It muffled their words and deadened their touch. Sometimes he suspected that in fact Sylvie already knew. He searched her eyes for signs of a hurt so deep that she had chosen to keep it to herself.

'What?' she asked. 'Have I got something in there? Am I getting a sty?'

Oz is talking about Kerran. They didn't keep in touch. 'He was a creep, anyway. And a bludger.'

Al uncaps another two bottles and remembers that the gourmet meals are not yet in the oven. With his back to Osmond he says, 'So Bron and Charlie — they're still together then.'

When Al turns around he sees that Osmond's eyes are screwed up as if in an effort of great concentration. 'Not exactly,' he finally decides. 'No.'

Al feels sure that Oz had already stated otherwise. 'Oh,' is all he can think of to say. He sits down.

'Bron, she got this scratch,' says Osmond. 'Climbing through a fence. Barbed wire. She got an infection.'

'Goodness! Bad?'

'Yeah. Pretty bad. Actually she died.'

Al takes a moment. 'That's terrible!' he says. He doesn't believe it. He doubts whether, in her whole life, Bron ever climbed through a fence.

Osmond's eyes are turquoise stones. 'They couldn't revive her,' he says.

He's watching Al closely, perhaps to see if Sylvie's husband will recognise that these were his very own words. There's something going on here. Something that Al can sense but can't get a grip on.

Sylvie would have known what it was, what to say, what to do.

'I'm sorry,' Al mumbles insincerely.

'Me too,' whispers Oz, and Al is shocked to see that those gemstone eyes are filling with tears.

Al gets up — without even giving it thought, as if this is the only possible thing to do — and puts his arms around Oz's trembling shoulders and his cheek against Oz's hard little earrings, and holds him.

FAME

He's about to come up before the Parole Board. Damon Baker. The name may not ring any bells, not anymore, but a few years back it would have. And I'm not talking Sunday bells, swaying and hollering out to the faithful. I'm talking alarm bells, trapped and frantically battering.

I like the way I've worded that. A metaphor, if I'm not mistaken. Twelve years ago Damon Baker was famous for murdering my sister-in-law, Leanne.

My de facto sister-in-law, to be strictly accurate. De-facto twice over since Leanne and Damon were not married and neither were Chrissie and I, though we'd talked about it. Chrissie wanted some kind of ceremony, but without her family present. It seemed easier to wait until we'd saved up enough to shift to Australia.

Maybe if we'd been married it would have held us together, but somehow I doubt it. Anyway, Damon Baker was, for a time, my de facto brother-in-law. And I have to admit to having told this to a number of people over the years, though increasingly I have to remind them about what he did. 'He was my brother-in-law,' I hear myself saying. Boasting, which, when you think about it, is weird. Like, I am related to this dude who hacked his girlfriend to pieces with a tomahawk, isn't that something?

I don't tell people I was related to Leanne, though of course they can figure that out. I don't usually think of myself as related to Leanne, though I guess I did at the time, when she was all that any of us could think about. Her body hacked open, her blood everywhere, her screams that the neighbours said didn't last very long or they probably would have gone to help. (Oh yeah, we said to each other.) Not even shouting, those neighbours said. It all happened very quietly, considering the mess.

Carnage was the word they used in the papers and on TV.

Why don't I want to connect myself with Leanne?

It's true that I didn't much like her, though this was mainly out of loyalty to Chrissie. The two had never had got along. Leanne was older than Chrissie, meaner than Chrissie and — though I swore otherwise — better looking than Chrissie. Leanne was, and had always been, their mother's favourite daughter. 'She loves herself,' Chrissie would hiss with her teeth clenched.

In that family, where rubbishing people was as natural as breathing, loving yourself was a major sin.

Chrissie was always a bit of a puzzle. She knew what her family was like and despised them for it. She wanted to get right away from them — she said so, over and over. Yet sometimes she wasn't much different from them.

If I pointed this out she'd turn right into her mother. What made me think my shit didn't stink? Did I have any inkling of what people thought of me? The things they would say behind my back? And on and on. So bad and so exactly like Loretta, such a perfect take-off, that I would have to laugh. After a bit Chrissie would be laughing too, but I never felt sure that laughter had been the outcome she'd intended.

So I didn't much like Leanne on Chrissie's behalf, but at the same time I wanted Leanne to like me. Or at least to be aware of me, if you know what I mean. And she was. Chrissie would no doubt say that this was just Leanne — she saw a man, any man, and she gave out signals. Always had done, always would do. And part of me believed that, but it didn't stop me liking this feeling that Leanne was aware of me and at the same time aware of herself. Her eyes would run over me like the smooth but unnerving end of a stethoscope, checking the state of my organs.

It was the same even when Damon came on the scene, so perhaps it was just Leanne's way, and nothing intended. But Damon didn't know that; you could tell by the way he'd watch her. You'd see him standing off to the side keeping Leanne in view while pretending not to. He was an inch or two shorter than she was, but good looking in a quiet kind of way. Solidly built — the type of guy who stands with his legs slightly apart, bracing himself. Not trusting the ground beneath him to stay in one place.

I've had to remember little details like that because people would ask me, what was he like — this monster I was related to? And there wasn't really a whole lot to say. In fact I met him only five times in the almost three years that he and Leanne were together. The first time, Leanne brought him round to our place, I think to show him off. Another three times were family occasions — a Christmas, a wedding and a funeral. The wedding was brother Shane's (Chrissie and Leanne's brother, not mine) and the funeral was for their cousin Jodi. She was seventeen. Jodi, her boyfriend and his Harley, all of them written off in one split-second.

Damon didn't smoke, at least not cigarettes, but Leanne did, so at these public affairs he'd be mostly hanging around outside on the edge of the smokers. He wasn't much of a talker — would leave it to you to start up a conversation or else just stand there with a nod or a smile when you caught his eye. Actually that smile is one thing I've never remembered to tell about him. It always took a while to get there, Damon's smile. But you would see it coming — a kind of ripple effect that would start with his eyes and work its way down, crinkling his cheeks and, finally, looping his mouth into a shining, lopsided half-moon. He had great teeth. That's another thing I've never before thought to mention.

The other time we met was when we ran into them one night outside the Coyote Bar. Leanne was keen we all go for a drink so we went down the road to a regular pub where the drinks were cheaper. Chrissie was teasing Damon about how quiet he was. After he made any little remark she'd say, 'Shut up, Damon. We're sick of you hogging the conversation,' or 'Off again. Rest of us can't get a word in edgeways.' The grin on his face that night was almost permanent and when we got home Chrissie said, 'She'll dump him soon, I guarantee. He's not her type — she can't stand nice.'

Later she swore she'd said no such thing. But she did. I remember feeling jealous.

What sort of stuff did Damon talk about? Well, there was dogs. Leanne had this bull terrier cross named Loco — but if you remember the case you'll know about that. Damon wasn't at all keen on Loco — he showed me the scar on his calf, the individual tooth marks — but he did like dogs in general. There was a labrador that he'd had as a kid; it used to go after cars. Finally his uncle or someone put the boot in to teach the dog a lesson, and did so much damage they had to have it put down.

He never said anything bad about Leanne, or even her family, though believe me there was plenty that could have been said. At the wedding dance I tried out a smart remark — this was after

43

Loretta had accused Albert's brother Ken of being a pervert and Shane had taken a swing at Albert and the bride's father had rung the cops. I said something sarcastic about how girls are supposed to turn into their mothers and what a treat we both had in store. But Damon wasn't buying into that — his face took on a look as though I was blaspheming. I knew that look only too well; my parents were both God-fearing. I grew up with the sense of the world being a prison yard — the Almighty up there in the tower with binoculars, watching your hands and reading your mind.

Now there's something we could maybe talk about, me and Damon, if we ever met up again.

It was at Jodi's funeral that Damon let out the only thing you might call a clue. He asked me if Chrissie played games with my head. Then, just a bit later, he said perhaps we should swap sisters, would I like that? I kind of laughed it off. I knew it wasn't a joke but I didn't know how to take it. Was he suspicious of me as regards Leanne? Did he fancy Chrissie? Was he unhappy with Leanne and looking for someone to talk to about their relationship? Or was that just his idea of the stuff men said to each other?

Over the years that's the conversation I've repeated to people. Not word for word, and sometimes, I admit, I've beat it up a few notches to make it seem more significant. I even, once, got carried away and made it sound as if for that moment Damon Baker had opened up and allowed me a glimpse of something dark and profoundly weird.

That is the Damon people want to know about. The one that fits the evidence at the trial and the wild-eyed photograph that the newspapers ran over and over again. The other Damon — the shy one with the dazzling girlfriend — he's nobody.

Damon Baker drowned the bull terrier, Loco, in the bath that Leanne had just stepped out of. That's what they said, and a thing like that stays in your mind. The thought of those small yellow eyes looking up through the water, the effort of forcing down all that sinew and muscle . . .

Why is it I claim kinship with the murderer but not with the victim? I've asked myself this and the honest answer is that murderers have a higher profile. They have done something of interest, whereas their victim has only died. Sick but true.

In life Leanne was much more interesting than Damon. Is he aware that he's turned the tables?

'Not a flicker,' fumed Chrissie after the first day of the trial. 'Not the tiniest little hint of emotion.' She was also angry that their father hadn't flown over from Alice Springs, not for the funeral or for the trial. 'Everyone else was there,' she said pointedly. Even Albert's son from a long-ago marriage. Everyone but the father and me. Chrissie couldn't understand why I wouldn't take leave from work and go with her. 'You owe it to Annie,' she said, and burst once again into tears.

Annie, it seems, was their pet name for Leanne, though up until then I'd heard no one use it. Leanne, dead and dismembered, turned into a saint. Loretta had the leggiest photo from her daughter's modelling portfolio transplanted onto a plate, which she hung on the living-room wall between the Mexican man on black velvet and the flat-backed vase of china violets. And Chrissie glued back the Leanne portion of the photo of the two of them in the Farmers' toy department with Santa, circa 1962.

It was this transformed version of Leanne that began the breakdown of Chrissie and me as a couple. Even though I soon gave up pointing out the inconsistencies, I'd apparently get 'that look' on my face. She accused me of not understanding her grief, she accused me of lack of feelings, she even accused me of having the potential to be another Damon. She spent more and more time at Loretta and Albert's place.

Leanne had been the favourite daughter; now Chrissie was

making up for lost time. That's what I thought but didn't say. Perhaps Chrissie was right and I was a heartless bastard.

I figured all this — the weeping and raging — would pass. I imagined it as a massive wave that had come pounding in, knocking us all around in different directions and degrees. I waited for it to sigh and slink away, for Chrissie to be once again my funny, clear-eyed darling.

Apart from the funeral I kept well clear of her family but they were still in my face. On the front page of the morning paper, on the TV screen. Leanne was gone and her family was news. First it was Albert, waving his ciggie and saying 'An eye for an eye,' while Shane stood in the doorway scowling. Next thing it was Loretta, with turquoise eyelids and her hair piled up in organised disarray. She talked about Leanne's modelling 'career', her hopes of being a fashion designer. 'She was the talent and heart of this family,' Loretta told the camera as her blue eyelids trembled and a couple of tears dribbled out.

Then Damon's sister from Taupo got in on the act. Their mother had died when Damon was four months old, and the children — three of them — had been fostered out. Damon had been through a number of foster homes before being adopted at the age of twelve.

Loretta and Albert went on a current affairs show to say that too many excuses were made for murderers. They had treated Damon like their own son. Let's get back, they said, to capital punishment or at least life sentences that really mean LIFE. Their loss, after all, would last a lifetime.

They were quite impressive, I have to admit. You could see that the TV people had done some work on Loretta's make up and Albert's choice of shirt.

Next thing Damon's brother pops up in Dunedin saying his sister has got it all wrong: Damon was not the youngest but the oldest child and would have been seven when the mother died. This brother had been told by an uncle that Damon, at four years old, had toppled from a window, landing head first on a concrete path.

It was hard to tell whether that last bit of information was supposed to add to our understanding of Damon, or whether the brother was just hard pressed for a personal memoir to contribute.

And so it went on. All the news clippings and video tapes (including the news footage of the funeral in which my left ear and shoulder featured briefly) were collected and stored in a wooden box on which the name ANNIE was written in small shells. I watched Chrissie gluing and placing those shells, the tip of her tongue pushed out in concentration, and I kept my own tongue firmly in its place.

The box was to go in the corner of Loretta's living room, part of a shrine she and Chrissie were putting together.

As you can imagine, the media attention, while it lasted, brought the family a fair degree of excitement. They'd be recognised in the street, total strangers would front up full of sympathy and admiration.

There was a bit of a lull before the trial. Chrissie went back to work, where she was, suddenly, more popular than Hamburger Heaven. She no longer stayed overnight at Loretta and Albert's, but brought her nightmares home to our bed. Screaming, some nights, without even waking. Still, I began to think we might be all right.

Then the trial began and we were back where we started. When I refused to go, Chrissie said that told her more about me than she'd learned in the five and a half years we'd been together. We gave it another few weeks, then I was the one who moved out. In fact I moved to another city. It was a relief, as if I wasn't so much leaving Chrissie as escaping Leanne.

That was twelve years back. Damon was sentenced to sixteen years. Now he's up for parole — it says so in the morning paper. Under the headline *Killer must stay behind bars* is a story about Loretta and Albert's submission to the Parole Board.

'Why should he go free when our beautiful daughter is gone forever?' demands Loretta. 'What kind of justice is that?'

I scan down to 'Leanne's younger sister, Christine, speaks often to daughters Sacha and Bridgette and about their Aunty Annie.'

No photo of Chrissie and kids. Just Loretta and Albert standing outdoors arm in arm like an ad for some retirement home. He's lost those last few threads of hair and a fair bit of weight but she looks exactly the same. Maybe the hair is now white instead of blonde but you really can't tell in a black and white picture.

Josh Fell, from the front office, is heading my way juggling coffee, a sugar bun and a folded newspaper. I clear a space for him. He slaps his paper down next to mine. 'What do you reckon? This parole business.'

'I don't know,' I say. 'I have no opinion.'

'You can't not have an opinion,' says Josh. 'I'll tell you what — he's butchered one woman, let him out and he'll do it again.' His finger stabs at the small photo of Damon Baker tucked down beneath all the print. It's that same stunned-eyed picture they were using twelve years ago. For once I have no inclination at all to claim a relationship. Not with Damon, nor with Leanne. I let Josh have his opinion. I look again at Loretta and, in the slant of her eyes and the curve of her top lip, I can see my Chrissie.

LEMONS

At the market you buy lemons. You walk slowly past the bundled fresh herbs, fat taro, buckets of shellfish, trays of exotic lentils, and settle for the cool, waxy familiarity of lemons. Seven. You drop them into your woven flax bag, smiling back at the woman who is perhaps not much older than you, yet heavy on her feet and unduly respectful. You look at her and you see that she has already stepped from the centre of life and now plods quietly towards extinction.

This thought makes you aware of your own fitness. Your neat tanned legs beneath the decently baggy shorts, the readiness of your body to respond to your requirements. The woman who smiles at you across the trestle table does not study herself in mirrors; her existence is confirmed in the eyes of others. You try to imagine how such a life must be, but there's no way in. You wonder what she thinks of you.

He looks up from his book. 'What did you get?'

You show him.

'Will we use all those?'

'We could take up gin,' you say. He knows you don't mean it — you've both sworn not to, no matter how hot or how tempting the twist of lemon, the clink of ice. Tropical gin drinkers are of a type you are not prepared to belong to.

'What else?' he asks as his eyes drift back to the book.

'Nothing.'

'Nothing we needed?' He directs the question at the open pages.

'It's just down the road. We can go back later.'

'All the best stuff will be gone.'

You place the lemons in a woven bamboo bowl with black stains inside. It's either that or the yellow plastic thing. You speak to him through the open door.

'I thought we might take the bus into town for dinner.' You're thinking steak, crisp on the outside, pale within, and thin fries and lettuce sliced up the way your mother still serves it, with hard-boiled eggs and a dollop of thick mayonnaise on the side.

You won't shame yourself by asking for this. The two of you will seek out a nice little place where the locals eat, and converse with the waiter as best you can. That's the kind of travellers you are.

You rub liniment on your calves, more out of habit than need. It's something to do. He's still in the shade with his book. You haven't finished the Amy Tan but you can't settle down and read, not yet. For five days you've walked, just the two of you with your lives on your backs, side by side and mostly in silence. Stopping at small villages and not sleeping soundly at night in case the smiling faces are just a mask for covetousness. (Though apart from the shared wallet that he wore on a strap even at night there was little to steal. Even your hiking boots were well worn and strictly utilitarian. Not because things might be stolen but because the flaunting of material possessions would be insensitive.)

fringe, the wife's face is a crescent moon: all nose and chin with a tight little mouth crushed between.

'She's very outgoing, your wife.'

'Sorry?'

You raise your voice. 'You're wife, she's very — '

'Full on.'

'Outgoing.'

'Same thing.' He smiles. 'I guess one of us needs to be.'

'So it doesn't bother you?' You're allowed to ask this. You're on holiday so the rules are different.

'You think it should?'

'No,' you assure him, feeling foolish. 'No, of course not.'

You can think of nothing else to say.

'We could see you two chatting up a storm,' says the wife and laughs. Your man throws you a grin but his eyes dart away before you can signal your wish to escape.

'Ask him about trains,' the wife instructs you. 'Trains and you can't shut him up. He's obsessed with trains. That's why we brought him here — they don't have any.'

The son laughs with her.

'I like trains,' you say, taking the husband's side since he isn't there to stick up for himself.

'Do you like trains?' she asks your beloved.

He throws you a glazed smile that you take to be an apology. 'They're not top of my list.'

You track his eyes to the small white teeth of the wife as they nibble at the slice of lemon she's fished from her gin.

'We've put it on plastic,' the husband tells you. 'We decided we might as well do it in style. You only live once.'

You follow his gaze out past the fresh concrete wall where scaffolding clings like seaweed. From the darkness beyond that wall comes the sighing of gentle surf — or perhaps what you hear is just the sibilant percussion sound of the music you left three floors below.

The son stayed down there on his mother's orders. 'Failing all else, chat up the girl behind the bar.'

The four of you left him hunched at a table beside the dance floor.

Your man has been summonsed inside to assist in the mixing of margueritas. They bought the makings duty free on the flight over, an economy measure. You promise yourself that after the margueritas you will insist on leaving. You could hear them in there clinking and laughing but not any more. You seem to have been waiting a very long time for the drinks. There is no reason why you should not go in and hurry things up.

'I think there's a boat out there,' he says as you go to rise. 'They'll be fishing, no doubt.' He stands up with you. On one side you have the balcony rail, on the other the husband. 'That small light, bobbing.' He points to the right of the concrete wall. You squint out into the darkness but can see no small bobbing light.

'How can we go home and leave all this?' he laments in a soft, sad voice.

You search for something cheerful to say. 'So you like boats too? As well as trains.'

'I hope I'm not quite as boring as she pretends.'

'Of course you're not,' you say unwillingly.

'You're not feeling cold, are you?' He touches your arm with limp fingers. You think of fish.

'No,' you say quickly, 'not cold.' Though suddenly you are.

'It's nice out here,' he says.

You step towards the curtained doorway. His hand returns to

your arm as if by way of restraint. 'We'll go in soon,' he says, but you push past him.

'Well, if you must.' He's right behind you.

The wife raises her head up, looks straight at you and smiles. Beyond that the picture is confused, as if your brain is delivering it as a collage. Her naked thighs, the veins on your darling's neck, her small teeth, his stifled groan, his smooth tanned knee, her big white thighs . . .

The husband slides his arms around you from behind. 'We're all on holiday,' he murmurs against your ear. You push the arms away but do not move. Your legs have forgotten how to function.

The husband steps in front of you, his hands at his sides.

'You must understand,' he tells you, 'that she and I have a dysfunctional relationship.'

You hang your bathing costume in the shade so the sun won't bleach out the blue and you walk back inside. His book lies on the table, spine up, and the unread section looks as thick as it did the day before.

He's sprawled on the top of the bed, asleep or pretending to be. You've not yet got used to the idea that things, with him, may not be what they seem. As you dress you imagine he's watching you through slitted peephole eyes. You toy with things you might say but, since the night before, the silences between you have been so busy it's hard to get a word in, never mind a fully constructed thought.

He waits until you're leaving the room.

'There's a funny smell. In the kitchen.'

You breath in experimentally. 'It's the waste bucket. One of those lemons was rotten.'

'I told you we wouldn't use them,' he says.

'I'll squeeze them,' you offer, 'and make us big long lemon

drinks.' But already you know that the distinctive smell of mouldy lemon is not coming from beneath the sink.

You prod with dismay at the fruit in the bowl. 'It's spread,' you tell him. 'Some are already furry and the rest have gone all soft and splotchy and pale.'

You wait for him to respond but there's nothing. You press your foot on the lever that opens the lid of the rubbish bucket and tip the decaying lemons from their discoloured bowl. Illogically you expect them to land with a clatter or even a tinkle. It's the sound you imagine this new kind of silence will make when you figure out how to break it.

'I guess it's the climate,' you say.

UNDYING

With the passage of years murder becomes understandable. At sixty-three Margot can think of a number of situations where a quiet dispatching would seem to be the sensible solution.

Take a marriage where the oppressed spouse waits for the other to die; that being the only alternative to the severely reduced circumstances both would suffer after a matrimonial split. Not to mention the trauma and public sense of failure that divorce entails. Margot knows all about this, having been twice divorced.

Twice the home she had struggled to provide for herself and her children has been wrenched from her and sliced in half in the name of justice. In fact the first husband, the father of her children, took more than half because he was a man and so was Margot's lawyer, and back then being a man was all that counted. He took his larger share of the proceeds from the sale of their house and left, with his fancy-woman, for Canada to avoid the burden of contributing towards his children's support.

Widowhood, Margot believes, is a blessed state. She remembers how it was in those long-ago daydreams — the ashen-faced ambulance attendants, the kindly doctor, the tears, the comforting hugs. Their wedding photo beside the coffin. How young they both looked, and how happy they were!

And the second husband? She should have known better. Well, what can be said, except that solo parenting makes for lonely evenings and he liked well-padded women and also children. The ready-made home and family he'd never had. And he was on an invalid's benefit, so Margot could go back to work.

A little too fond of the children it seemed, though it took her friend Val to point this out. Bad touching. (Which, frankly, had been what Margot liked most about him. She was available for as much of that as he liked.)

There was really nothing to go on but Val's instincts and the brick that lodged in Margot's gut, substantial enough to be accepted as proof. She needed him out, and fast. Half the house seemed a small enough price to pay, at least at the time. No fuss on condition he stayed well away.

She's seen him, though, at Northlands Mall. He was with an emaciated young woman and two little girls. Margot considered following them home and warning the woman, but it wasn't as if there was any real evidence.

If he'd died, there would have been no such dilemma, and she'd still be living in her dear little cottage, with the mortgage all but paid off.

On the other hand, when Val got into that Wicca nonsense, with secret meetings where they danced about all naked as jays, Margot had begun to have a few qualms about Val's credibility.

She has no doubts, however, about the two-faced bitch her first husband ran off with. This was a woman who had pretended to be

Margot's friend throughout the year-long affair that preceded the divorce. And yes, Margot knows it takes two, but men are easily led and when it comes to a choice between two o'clock feeds and nappies drying in front of the fire and Schubert and chardonnay in a city apartment overlooking the park — well, really there is no contest.

Margot had heard, indirectly, that the relationship fell apart within their first year in Toronto. She was gratified but unsurprised. A woman so lacking in conscience will do the same thing again and again. Her premature demise would have saved a number of people a great deal of pain.

But Margot is not one for regrets. She has no time for people who sit around whining. You get off your arse and get on with your life — that's what she used to tell her children. And if you make mistakes, make sure you learn from them.

Margot's mistakes have been due to bad judgement. It runs in the family (which is not an excuse, but an observation). Margot's father had very poor judgement. He married, got his wife pregnant, then rushed off to fight a war on the other side of the globe. And Margot's mother, instead of staying home and raising her child, left baby Margot in the care of her parents and signed up as a landgirl; perhaps from patriotic duty but more probably because landgirls had more fun. And Margot's mother did, it seems, have a little fun before the caterpillar tractor overturned and crushed her to death.

Margot has been told that her mother, when she died, was four months pregnant.

This information is suspect, since it came from her father's second wife and was conveyed only once, by way of prognosis.

'You'll turn out to be a slut just like your mother. Yes, that got your attention, didn't it, madam? No sooner were you born than your mother went off and got herself up the duff to some high-country farmer. Who already had a wife. Yes, miss smarty-pants.

There's something you didn't know.'

Only in recent years has Margot begun to wonder if perhaps her mother's death was not the result of carelessness or random misfortune. Where was the high-country farmer when the tractor rolled? Where was the farmer's wife?

Every day, Margot supposes, people are getting away with murder. Oh, not the young ones with their hidden eyes and rifle collections and army surplus clothes disguised as tropical undergrowth. (As if there's a rule that wars may not be conducted in cities, or snow, or deserts.) Those young men, driven by unspeakable rage at their lack of importance, get captured and make the headlines as intended. You need to be middle-aged or older to kill discreetly. You need to have weighed things up, considered the greater benefit to mankind, to be certain that this is your best or only solution.

These are Margot's thoughts as she stacks the shelves with cans of beetroot, sachets of instant coconut cream and packets of pancake mix. She no longer notices the shoppers milling around her, but she is aware of the food she arranges in single and double rows. She'd supposed that looking at food all day would put her off it, but no such luck.

Once, way back in the first marriage, Margot dug up a rats' nest — the real thing — in the middle of her compost heap. The mother rat had fled, so what Margot's spade unearthed was a cluster of babies — small, white, blind, snub-nosed creatures, not rat-like at all. In fact they looked like miniature hippopotamuses.

She was at a loss as to what she should do. Allow them to die slowly of hunger? Dispose of them quickly? Flush them? Bury them? Not while they're still alive!

In the end she tipped them onto the concrete step, found a rock and smashed it down. Amazingly, at least two survived that first attack. Her stomach heaved. She smashed the rock down repeatedly, not looking, then scraped the mess up with the spade and delivered it back to the compost heap, hoping the mother rat would not recognise that porridge of flesh and entrails as her massacred babies. Then Margot went back and scrubbed the step.

In nightmares the baby rats returned, the two who had at first survived and their mangled siblings. Sometimes their mother came with them, lips rolled back and teeth like yellow needles.

Margot buys tickets at the Lotto counter beside the main doors but never wins anything. This is as she expects but that doesn't stop her from buying more tickets. If she won she would divide the money between her children, not in equal parts but according to need and effort.

The oldest child is diligent but possibly suffers from inherited lack of judgement. The small business she'd worked so hard to establish has run into serious debt due to one light-fingered employee. Now Margot's daughter runs the business alone, working all hours just to pay off the interest on her extended bank loan. In the event of a Lotto win Margot would help her oldest child. Also her son, who has been diagnosed with muscular sclerosis. Margot tries not to think about his future in the hands of an overstretched public health system. Should she sell her small back-unit home to pay for private medical care?

In Margot's opinion the news of her son's illness ought to have brought his twin scuttling home, but it didn't. She lives in Scotland with her Norwegian partner, and hasn't been home in seven years. If this daughter has problems she doesn't convey them to Margot. She would get some of the Lotto money, but not much.

It was when she was told what was wrong with her son that Margot began thinking about the merits of murder.

Her father's major lapse of judgement was, of course, in marrying Noeline. She used to come into his shop to look at drapes and umbrella stands, so Margot's father knew her by sight, but nothing was happening until he won second prize in the Art Union and they ran his photo in the local paper. After that Noeline must have come in quite a lot. Sometimes she was still there in the late afternoons when Margot was hanging around after school.

Margot didn't pay the woman much attention, though she noticed the nice shoes and big, glittery earrings. So when her father asked what did she think of his new friend, he had to describe her so Margot knew who he meant.

'The pretty one,' her father had said, going pink. 'With the yellow hair and the lovely smile.'

Margot still couldn't place her, and even at seven years old she knew this wasn't a promising start.

'Never mind.' He patted her head.

And suddenly Margot knew. 'Earrings. Dangly ones and other ones. And high shoes, with straps and things.'

'That's her,' said her father with visible relief. 'That's good. I knew you two would get along.'

And before Margot could say 'Snow White' her father and Noeline had got married in a registry office while Margot was in school getting a gold star for sums. And before Margot could say 'Hansel and Gretel' Noeline was replacing their cosy furniture with fat shiny stuff from the showroom of the shop.

Margot no longer went there after school; she went home to Noeline and peeled potatoes and folded the washing and cleaned her father's shoes. Her father came home later and later; he no longer had just the one shop but a chain of shops, and most days he worked at Head Office on the other side of the city. Noeline was awfully nice to Margot's father on account of him being lumbered with a stupid and lumpy child.

Margot spent less time with her friends because Noeline said they were the wrong types. Mostly she stayed in her room doing things that changed as the years progressed:

putting paper outfits on cardboard dolls

reading Georgette Heyer and *My Friend Flicka*

imagining what happened with boys

reading Peyton Place and almost knowing

painting her face with watercolours to get the idea

wondering if Paul Jordan liked her

squeezing her pimples and shaving her legs

writing stuff in her diary, in code in case Noeline found it

The day after she turned sixteen Margot left home and school. Her father was upset. There was a scene. Margot said, 'She hates me,' Noeline's husband said, 'Don't be silly,' and Noeline said, 'How can you do this to your father?' Then she said to him, 'You see what I mean? When you're not here this is what I get. Day after day.'

Margot didn't go to visit. She met the first husband and they moved to another city. Margot posted off a card giving their new address. Each Christmas they sent her a present (soaps or hand-cream or a chemist voucher) and a letter that began 'Dear Friends, Well another year has passed — too quickly . . .' In return she sent off presents that could be for both of them (tablemats, towels, candlesticks) and a Christmas card on which she noted such major events as the arrival of children and the departure of husbands.

Sometimes Margot's news was acknowledged in a return letter from her father, along with complaints about the difficulty of finding things in their latest house.

Only when the tumour they'd removed from his left leg turned out to be malignant did her father fly up to visit. He booked himself into a hotel downtown and asked her to meet him there. Her children had all left home years earlier but she took along photos.

He had become an old man. He held her hands and wept and

63

said he was sorry, he didn't know how they could have grown so far apart. Then he said he was aware that Noeline had made things difficult.

'She's not really the motherly type,' he said.

And Margot had sat on the sofa in that cavernous, almost empty foyer and felt the understatement swell in her throat until she could hardly breathe.

'I want you to remember me this way,' he said. 'I mean, don't come down to watch me die.'

'I doubt if she'd let me,' said Margot.

'You'll be taken care of,' he said. 'I promise you that. Noeline's no longer young and doesn't keep good health. I hope you'll see your way to remembering me as someone who did look after you. In his way.' And he gave her a rueful smile.

She went down by train for the funeral. The church was crowded with people who worked for her father's company, and the minister seemed uncertain about the nature of the man he was farewelling. Far-sighted, he said in a voice that invited contradiction, and hard working. A captain of industry. Margot sat in a back pew surrounded by strangers. Noeline sat up the front with her only surviving sister. She looked a little smaller than Margot remembered. Slim and expensive and composed.

Margot received a letter from her father's lawyer, along with a copy of the will. The letter advised that Noeline was a life beneficiary of her husband's estate. When she died the assets would transfer to Margot.

Noeline was, at that time, eighty-two.

I can wait, Margot had told herself. She imagined visiting Scotland with her oldest daughter and her son who, at that time, was in perfect health.

That was nine years ago.

The thought crossed other people's minds. 'We'd need a definite timeframe,' said the Loans Manager. 'You couldn't, perhaps, give her a small shove at the top of the stairs?'

'Ground glass,' said Val. 'I'll lend you my mortar and pestle.'

This was when they were still best of friends. Before the witches, and the falling out.

'Try prising your mind open, even just a tiny fraction,' said Val.

'Or you'll put a spell on me?'

'As I already said, we only do good stuff.'

'Like?'

'Like . . . making sure someone you love has a really good year, or makes a wise decision.'

'Kind of hard to measure.'

'Get stuffed,' said Val.

Their argument pestered Margot's mind as she stacked baked beans and unloaded tinted pasta. She mused, especially, on her own words: *kind of hard to measure.* Never had Margot read or heard of a murder trial in which the evidence pointed to death by witchcraft. Which probably just proved her contention that it was a load of hogwash.

But if Margot opened her mind a tiny fraction . . .

In her lunch break Margot browsed the arcade bookshop and discovered to her dismay that there must be masses of Vals out there, prancing about in bodies that witches surely deserve and providing a market for a variety of little books with titles like *100 Helpful Spells and Wicca for Universal Harmony.* Margot flicked through the pages: moons and tides and twigs and candles and herbs and incense. No help at all.

On her day off Margot went to the library. The young woman at the help desk looked at her with distaste and pointed. 'That corner there. But you won't find much; it's always out.' She curled her lip. 'It's the most popular section in the library.'

'It's just for research,' said Margot hastily. 'It seems there are all these white witches about.'

'Not just white ones.' The librarian leaned forward conspiratorially. 'We've given up replacing the Aleister Crowley. It's stolen every time. It's our most stolen book ever.'

Margot wasn't familiar with Aleister Crowley and nothing in the corner looked very promising. She flipped through *Powers of Evil* and *The Encyclopedia of Ancient and Forbidden Knowledge* but they weren't any help. If there were voodoo books they were all on loan and anyway wax dolls were, surely, too much of a cliché to be taken seriously.

Next time she found herself in the bookshop Margot took a closer look at the little gift books for wannabe witches. She imagined Val in a Wicca circle burbling out those incantations, making a tit of herself.

Borrow a personal item from the recipient of your charm or spell, the little books instructed Margot.

So much for that idea.

Three days later a letter comes from the Tranquillity Retirement Home where Noeline is spending her days and her late husband's money. 'Dear Margot, Your mother has requested we write to you. As you will know, her arthritis has rendered her unable to write herself. She wishes to speak with you on a matter of urgency, and asks that you visit as soon as you possibly can.'

After a few moments of indignation over that 'mother', Margot feels a surge of joy and relief.

Obviously (finally) Noeline is dying, and knows it. In the short time left she'll be wanting to clear her conscience, repent, prise open those heavenly gates. There had been a time, Margot recalls, when Noeline had got religion, insisting on grace before meals and filling the house with small expensive icons.

Will Margot refuse Noeline absolution? Or, softened by the delight of what lay in store, was she prepared to forget and forgive?

Still undecided, Margot flies south on plastic money. She takes a taxi from the airport to Tranquillity. She has already rung the office to advise them that she is coming.

Noeline is in her apartment watching TV. She has shrunk considerably, and her hair has receded but the eyes are bright, giving her face a snake-like quality.

'So you came,' she says. 'I'll bet you thought I was on my last legs.'

Margot can feel her own face contracting and the years winding back.

'Well, don't just stand there with that idiotic look. Sit down.' Noeline points to an upholstered Queen Anne chair. Margot stumbles to it on thirteen-year-old hockey-playing legs, and sits on the edge just as she used to.

'So how long are you here for?'

'I go back tomorrow,' mumbles Margot to the carpet. 'If you stay overnight the tickets are cheaper.'

'Where are you staying?'

'The YMCA.'

Noeline shakes her head, raising a hand to half cover her smile. Margot, noting that the hand is knobbly and misshapen, feels confused.

'It's supposed to be quite nice,' she says. Her voice sounds girlish and unfamiliar.

'What time is your flight?'

'Nine o'clock.'

'That won't do. I need you in the morning. You can ring from here and change the booking. Phone's right there beside you. Dial one to get out. Do you have your ticket? The airline number will be on it.'

Margot has crawled back into a space where obedience is

automatic. She finds the ticket, dials, changes the flight.

'Right.' Noeline's voice has softened. This, too, is familiar. 'Can you be here by nine in the morning? I have an appointment in town and you have to come with me. We'll take a taxi.' She smiles — Margot imagines the flick of a forked tongue. 'It's regarding a matter that very much concerns you.'

Somewhere deep within Margot her matronly self is tapping for attention, but she is thirteen and despised: what can she do?

When she arrives the next morning Noeline is still in the bathroom applying her makeup. She calls through the door in a cheerful voice that she won't be long.

Margot looks around the immaculate and compact apartment. On a shelf, in a silver frame, is a photograph of her father. Next to it is a small porcelain statue that Margot remembers as belonging to Noeline's religious phase. A personal item? Possibly not. But Noeline's shoes are now clicking across the bathroom tiles so Margot snatches up the little statue and thrusts it into her pocket.

In the taxi Noeline chats as if they are friends. Margot knows better, yet is unable to stop herself from feeling grateful. The driver delivers them into the heart of the city. Margot notes the Casino, like a landed spacecraft. Noeline points to a café. 'You can meet me there.'

Margot watches her stepmother walk away: her upright carriage, her precise steps, her peacock-blue silk scarf flapping. She might live for years.

At a café table Margot examines the figurine and remembers that she always thought it ugly. Jesus sagging on a moss-covered cross and a young woman kneeling and gazing upwards. The folds in the back of her white robe hint at the sprouting of wings.

Noeline is sure to notice its absence.

Margot waits. Finishing her coffee she returns to the counter and examines the food on display. It is enticing and expensive. She chooses a macaroon because it costs less than everything else. She waits some more — a long time, with growing unease. She leaves the café and looks in doorways and entranceways: doctors, dentists, accountants, tax agents, solicitors. She has no idea where to begin. She returns to the café and buys a flat white, keeping an eye on the door.

It takes a few moments for recognition to take place. This woman who sweeps into the room with her bobbed hair and frothy silk scarf . . . Margot's entrails chill before her brain registers Noeline. For it is Noeline, it has to be — Noeline at thirty-something: the age at which she married, the height of her powers.

'It took less time than I thought,' she says, bearing down on Margot. She shows her teeth in what could be a smile. 'What's the matter? You look like a stunned mullet.' She laughs.

Noeline's neck, above the scarf, is as smooth as marble; the hands that pull out the chair across from Margot are manicured and unlined Margot feels a movement in the pocket that rests on her thighs. A kind of trickle.

'That's right!' Noeline glitters with triumph. Her eyes reflect red, like a flashlight photo, though it could be a trick of the light. 'I told you I had a transaction to arrange. It went rather well, don't you think? I needed you here to see for yourself. For a woman your age you're not in good shape. At best you've got . . . what? Twenty years? I wouldn't want you to waste it by living in hope.'

Margot's hand gropes in her pocket where the figurine was. Her fingers encounter only powdery sand. She is not surprised. Her own lack of surprise is the thing she finds most dismaying.

'You and your friends,' Margot tells Val, 'are toddlers, paddling and dabbling at the edge of an ocean. You're fools, you have no idea what's out there.'

As Val has remarked to the rest of the coven, Margot's mind, these days, is so wide open it's liable to fly off its hinges.

SLANT SIX

He sat for a long time, that night I met him, on the edge of things. A few people drifted over to talk to him. Once I would have been among them, worried that he might feel excluded. The instinct arose but I pushed it aside, telling myself in a Phil kind of voice, You're not responsible for the human race. You are not God, you are only Louise.

I've been doing my best to keep that thought in mind. Phil promised a feeling of lightness and joy, and I'm sure that will come as soon as I've learnt to deal with the guilt. The guilt is, of course, totally irrational. It's not as if I was brought up Catholic. It took Phil years and years to get beyond all that nonsense. Guilt is inextricably tied to the notion of original sin. Protestants, not being brainwashed into considering themselves personally responsible for the human condition, are saved the burden of abstract guilt.

When Phil first explained this I told him it sounded like a

rather Catholic view of things. And besides, what about me? I was never a Catholic. Not even a Protestant. I was nothing — not even agnostic since that seemed to imply some kind of position. Heathen I'd allow: it sounded staunch.

'Staunch!' Phil squeaked. 'Is that how you see yourself?' He began grinning up at the ceiling, savouring this evidence of my capacity for self-delusion.

'What about me?' I reminded. 'If you're so right, how come I'm . . . you know . . . ?'

'A mug.'

'Socially responsible.'

'A pushover.' He shrugged. 'Maybe you were Catholic in a previous life.'

Anyway, back to Dee's barbeque and my eventual meeting with Chip. Chip! I tried to constrain a Protestant grin but he must have seen it.

'I gather that, in this country, it is considered a stupid name.' Except he said *stoopid*. His voice was straight off a red-neck country album.

'Well,' I consoled him, 'at least it's not Randy.'

'Randy is worse?'

'Depends,' I said.

'Depends on what?'

'Don't go there,' said Dee, who was suddenly with us. She was shaking her head in warning or disbelief and behind my back her fingers nudged a signal I wasn't sure how to read.

Her mouth said to me, 'So, down south tomorrow. You all packed up and ready? Bet you can't wait.' She was smirking. Her hip whacked mine. 'You know what they say about hunger being the best sauce.'

'It's not that long,' I began to object.

A hand reached past my ear and handed Dee the cordless

phone. She pressed it against her bristled head, squinting, then moved away. I was left with Chip and the little-boy smile he'd worn all night. Only now it might be there on account of my sex life.

Certainly it seemed to have widened.

'Down south?' he said. 'Would that be –'

'Queenstown? Nope.'

'Why'd you say that? You guessed I was going to ask for a ride.'

'You weren't?'

'Maybe. But did I say I was going to Queenstown?'

'It was your shades,' I told him.

'My glasses? What's wrong with my glasses? They happen to be very expensive.' And he took them off to examine them in the bluish glow of Dee's garden lighting. His eyelashes were like tassels caught in a breeze. They caused me to reconsider the rest of him. Long legs in buff-coloured cargos slung fashionably low, a black t-shirt that said, in writing so small you had to be up close, I think therefore I think I am. Black and green trainers, almost new.

'That's what I mean,' I said. 'And also, if you hadn't noticed, it's dark.'

'And that's okay in Queenstown but not in Christchurch? Is that what you're saying?'

Dense or just American? I don't want to sound prejudiced, but they're just not good at making connections. They like the conversational path to be clearly marked, with edges — or better, a handrail. Who hasn't noticed? They grow anxious over anything left to the imagination. You see it on TV — the way they'll snatch up a sentence and dissect it without having even considered it as a whole. As if the way the words hung together was of no significance.

'Am I right? Is that what you're telling me?'

'Something like that,' I mumbled. Whatever I'd said, and already I couldn't remember, it wasn't intended for analysis or the *Oxford Book of Quotations*.

'I thought I'd stick to the coast,' he said. 'Dunedin. Have I got that correct? Yeah? And that's the route you're taking?'

My nod was infinitesimal. The kind of nod that could not be mistaken for an invitation.

'Well, there's a coincidence.'

I nodded again, taking steps backwards until the words on his t-shirt were just a ragged white smear.

He raised his voice. 'How are you travelling?'

'Car,' I said. 'My boyfriend's.' And I turned away to hide my delight at having won simply by telling the truth.

Chip came after me. 'Would he mind? Your boyfriend? One extra passenger. Shall I ask him? Is he here?'

'Is who here?' Min's glance slid across me and onto Chip. Over jeans she was wearing an old red petticoat with sagging lace. The kind of look Phil hated.

'Her boyfriend,' Chip said.

'He's in Dunedin,' Min said.

'Ah,' said Chip.

'She's going down to be with him. First thing in the morning.'

'Okay,' Chip said to me. 'I get it. You're driving his car down.'

'Thanks very much,' I told Min. She looked confused.

It was Chip who caught on. So much for national stereotyping! 'You want to travel alone,' he said. 'That's cool. I understand.'

'It's not that,' I said too quickly. For it was exactly that. It was three years since rust had taken my little old Mazda. I could have replaced her but, as Phil pointed out, there wasn't much point. Public transport was cheaper and better for the planet and if I needed a car there was his.

I didn't need one — except sometimes in the weekends, when Phil would be there to drive me. Then he went off to do his year on section at Windmouth High School and the car, of course, went with him. So it was, you could say, a bit of luck for me when the old

73

guy in the van backed into it because it got me this trip. He hit the wrong pedal and wham, right there in my local Pak 'N' Save car park with seven people who immediately offered their names as witnesses.

Phil had to go back on the shuttle. He was gutted, actually. He'd just got the tapedeck fixed and on the way to Pak 'n' Save he'd brought two talking books: *Mansfield Park* and *Gormenghast*. Just for the pleasure of re-acquaintance.

There had been a delay over parts and a complication concerning insurance, but I'd finally got to collect the car that morning. The thought of looking over the wheel at the open road, my feet massaging the pedals, brought a certain taste to my mouth. It was a kind of thirst but I thought of it as greed. I was so greedy to get on that road I was salivating.

I'd spent the previous evening taping Greg Brown. Three tapes would get me there. Nearly five hours of captivation.

'You don't trust me?' Chip was saying. 'I understand. Why should you? I could be some kind of crazy man.'

I shook my head, compelled (by some forgotten but pious existence?) to reassure. 'I'm . . . not definitely going. Not tomorrow . . . it depends on . . . a number of things.'

'No worries,' said Chip. 'Another day or so is fine with me. I don't have a schedule.' He delved in a kneeside pocket and produced a flashy ballpoint. 'I'll take down your number and give you a call first thing tomorrow to see what gives. If that's okay?'

He wrote my phone number on his inner arm, which was unexpectedly pale. I could have rearranged a couple of digits but I told myself no worries: he'd shower first thing and that would be that: I'd be gone. And anyway it was easy to lie on the phone. Trip's off, I'd say. I've changed my mind.

Later that night Phil rang. I must leave early to beat the traffic. Had I checked the tent pegs? Had I remembered the gas bottle? I should ask for an extra couple of days' leave.

'Stuff the job,' he said. 'You don't even like it, and there's heaps of things you could do down here.'

I was thinking what I should say.

'This is so like you,' he said. 'The negativity thing. Don't do this, Lou. Don't do this to yourself.'

Phil wanted us to live together on a forever basis. He wanted a baby, maybe two or three babies. These weren't things he'd cared about when we lived together before but distance had allowed him to see life more clearly.

Chip was waiting on the footpath outside the hostel. Beside him was a serious backpack and a bulging flax kete. It was necessary to rearrange the contents of the boot — the camping gear, the carton of essential grocery items, my small suitcase of clothes. I'd left the ignition on; Greg was singing his '64 Dodge song. Chip, I thought, will like this. He'll relate.

Chip offered to drive. I roared, 'No way!'

'Hey, I only meant — if you get tired.'

He folded himself into the passenger seat, then adjusted it back so far he was almost behind me. He could pull out a gun and I wouldn't know until I felt cold steel against my neck. Right away he began to tell me about Rotorua. 'I've been there,' I said, but it didn't deter him.

Just past Templeton I adjusted the sound dial upwards and pointedly hummed along. Chip's voice just grew louder. Near Rolleston there was a momentary pause and I took advantage. 'I love this man,' I said. 'You know him? He's from . . . I think it's Minneapolis, somewhere like that.'

'I don't know a single person from Minneapolis.'

'I meant did you know *of* him. He writes these fabulous songs. He's a poet, then also he's got this voice that is just so . . .'

75

'Country,' said Chip. 'Willie Nelson and stuff. I know country. Can't say I'm actually a fan or anything. But my aunt, she has this shop . . .'

We were now clear of the satellite towns and the low cloud that pressed down on the city like a migraine. Now it was all blue skies and clouds like skittering tufts of sheep's wool. I'd packed the wrong sort of clothes. I'd spend the week sweating and fanning, definitively uncool. If I was alone I could have turned around and gone home to repack. The dashboard clock said 11.43 and there wasn't another vehicle in sight. So much for needing to beat the traffic.

'Shall I tell you about the girl I left behind?' said Chip.

'No,' I told him.

That cracked him up. 'I love the way you came out with that. "Shall I tell" . . . "NO." That cracks me up. Just for that I am gonna tell you.' And he turned Greg down.

He turned Greg down. Reached out from behind me — a long freckled arm — and muted Greg Brown right in the middle of 'Lately'.

Why had I agreed to his coming? Why, despite common sense and various totally rational reservations, had I turned myself into a public transport service?

My mother once told me (preparing the ground for Phil) that I was either a fool or an optimist. Her tone implied that they were the same thing. I knew lots of people who would agree with her — Phil was one of them. And I could see that there were benefits and protections in thinking like that, which is why I was trying to change. But I didn't want, ever, to believe that hope and random acts of kindness were evidence of personal defects or outright stupidity.

It was true that, shortly after that phone conversation with Phil, a brief movie had flashed past my mind's eye. In that movie Phil was waiting outside the house where he rents the sleepout, and I pulled up. And there alongside me in the passenger seat, all long legs and classy shades, was Chip. Close-up of Phil's face. To be continued . . .

But, concerning Chip, the main thing was that it would've seemed unreasonable *not* to take him. I had seats to spare, Chip had a journey to make, and the planet was running out of resources.

As I had detoured into town to pick him up it seemed to make good sense. I thought of myself as a kind Kiwi and that gave me a little glow of pride. I thought of myself as belonging to a nation full of intrinsically decent people. Okay, perhaps a nation full of insecure people who want to be liked. Is that so bad?

Then people like Chip come along and take advantage, not even aware that that's what they're doing. It's a matter of type and perceptions. Kiwis come in small print with plenty of space for whatever's between the lines, while Yanks are all bold typeface and everything there on the page, spelt out in capitals.

I wanted to whip the red and orange cap right off Chip's head, ball it up and shove it down his throat. I wanted to bundle him into the boot with his designer backpack. Yet it wasn't his fault, nor was it mine.

I could pull over and say, 'Chip, get out, piss off, I'm not gonna hear about your girlfriend.'

'Why?' he'd say. 'What's wrong? Don't you like me? Have you no interest in other people's stories? I'm telling you, that's a sad way to be. I wouldn't've taken you for that kind of person. Not for a minute.'

And, since it felt like I'd had that conversation already, I couldn't stand to go through it again.

We crossed the Rakaia Bridge with Greg still reduced to a sibilant whisper; I couldn't even pick up which songs I was missing. Chip was onto the ex-girlfriend's stepfather's purebred wolves. I had to shout above him. 'This,' I hollered, 'is the longest bridge in New Zealand.'

77

My impression was that Chip had, so far, barely glanced out the window. Okay, the immediate countryside was kind of flat and featureless, but look to the right and there were the alps, blue-grey with distance and sprinkled with fresh snow. The guy was a tourist, for God's sake; it was his duty to look.

The wolf story faltered. 'That right?' said Chip, and actually heaved his body towards the window to look down at the riverbed. At the tangled pattern of rivulet channels, all of them dry, dry, dry, though it was not yet summer. 'How long is this bridge then?'

'I've no idea.'

'Approximately how long?'

'It probably says. If you keep an eye out.'

But already he had lost interest. In the bridge and also the wolves.

'I was maybe too old for her. I guess that was it. She was only just seventeen.' He paused, and I could feel his eyes on my neck, waiting for a response, or at least a reaction. He was proud of seventeen.

'There are more long bridges to come,' I said. 'This is wide-river country.' I wondered if that had ever been used as a song title. I could send it to Greg, but perhaps he would think it cheesy. The thing about Greg Brown — the thing I loved most of all — was, listen to any song on any album and you just knew that this was a man who believed in hope and random acts of kindness.

'Seen one river,' said Chip, patting his pockets, 'you've seen 'em all.'

When he held out a packet of gum I shook my head. I wanted to chew, my mouth felt like an unwashed teatowel, but even one piece of gum might compromise the purity of my dislike.

What was I thinking? One pellet of gum compared with around four hundred kilometres of travel. Who ought to be feeling indebted? But perhaps he would put in for petrol when I stopped to fill up. I should've made that a condition, right from the outset, but you kind of hope people will offer. That way it's nicer. That way you can both feel good about it.

Truth was, I didn't want him to offer. If he did I might even refuse. I wanted to seethe and press my foot down a little harder. Get the trip over and done with.

'What's this place? Are we coming into a city? Are we?'

'No, Chip. A town. And that was it; we're now on the way out.'

'I thought . . . you know . . . outer suburbs. You got a roadmap?'

'Nope.'

'Hey, come on, you gotta have a roadmap!'

'You're the one who doesn't know where he's going — why don't you have a roadmap?'

'I'm not the driver. If I was driving I'd'a stopped off and got me a roadmap.'

It was round about then, as we were leaving Ashburton, that I first noticed the smell. Freezing works, I thought, or something industrial. But it seemed to be travelling with us. A fart. Which explained why Chip had failed to remark on it. Silent and violent, as we said at primary school. Chewing gum does that, I've noticed: fills you with air. He must, surely, be mortified. I bit back a grin.

'I will have a gum,' I said. The stink felt like some kind of authorisation.

'Got some bad news,' said Chip. 'There was only three bits left and they're in my mouth. Ha ha ha.'

I wished I'd been nicer to that grin, kept it hanging around. The smell was still there. I was shallow breathing.

'Tell you what,' said Chip. 'Next gas station we stop and I'll buy you a packet. How far d'you reckon to the next gas station? There was one just back there a way, if you want to turn around?'

'Don't worry, ' I told him, 'I can live without.'

It seemed the smell was subsiding. I turned up the volume. Greg was likening modern love to a loaded gun. Phil wasn't a fan. In his book Greg Brown was a Luddite who had penned a couple of decent tunes and some deeply depressing lyrics. But Greg sang on and Chip showed no sign of becoming depressed. He began to whistle, though not at all tunefully.

'You recognise that? A hummingbird. You familiar with the hummingbird?'

'Only the movie, with Gregory Peck.' The clock said we'd been travelling just over an hour. Barely quarter of the way.

The smell had returned, even stronger, yet still he said nothing. He'd gone silent so now I felt sorry for him. I suffered, on his behalf, the random, clenching agony of a dodgy gut. I looked out for trees that he could crouch behind. Worried about how far it was to a public toilet.

Why did he still say nothing? Wisps of mist were drifting past the side window. Out of the bonnet. The arrow on the heat gauge had left H way behind.

This is a wonderful country. In the forty minutes we spent on the verge of the highway four drivers stopped with offers of help. The first gave us water for the radiator. A one-litre bottle of Sparkling Spring Water with the seal unbroken.

'We can't take that,' protested Chip.

'Yes we can,' I said, snatching it up.

I offered to pay for it but the owner refused. He was peering down at the volcanic engine. 'You will wait till it's cool,' he said, 'won't you?'

'He thought we were real dumb,' said Chip resentfully as the man drove off.

'I wonder why!' I snapped. My anger was at myself — how could I have let this happen? I was the kind of driver who kept an eye on her dials.

The second would-be Samaritans were heading for Dunedin with empty seats in the back. 'You go,' I begged Chip. But he wouldn't — he just couldn't — leave a woman alone on the highway. The couple entirely agreed.

Chip used his cap to open the radiator, even though I kept saying wait. A blast of steam and Chip leapt back but not quite fast enough. We poured the Sparkling Spring Water on the scalded arm. We had no option: it was all we had. The open radiator was repeatedly groaning and billowing up water and steam. 'Like Rotorua,' said Chip. 'Even the smell.'

My mind kept escaping back to before Ashburton, when life was so much better than I'd given it credit for.

A raisin-faced old guy with a vanload of kids pulled up. He crossed the road shaking his head. 'Never should take off the cap, not till it cools. And the ignition — gotta keep it running. Never should'a switched it off.' His eyes rested redly, but not unkindly, on Chip. 'Didncha know that?'

'I wasn't the driver,' said Chip. His cheeks had flushed up. 'If I'd been the driver we wouldn't be sitting here now.'

I reached for the keys. 'So I should turn it on?'

'I'd say so' The man looked from me to Chip and back again. He thought we were a couple. The thought appalled me. I had just cooked Phil's motor and there I was worrying about a stranger thinking Chip was my boyfriend.

I turned on the key and the motor started at once, which seemed like a good sign. Greg's voice leapt out to stroll the flat paddocks. I began to feel a little better.

Chip had thrown himself down on the grass and was examining his scalded arm. I thanked the man for his kindness in having stopped, and for his advice, and he waggled his head and walked back to the van full of kids. Then he walked back again with a couple of two-litre plastic containers full of water.

'Still far too hot.' He put the containers beside the bumper and stared at the engine.

'What d'you think?' I asked.

He shrugged. 'Might be lucky.'

The kids waved as he drove off. Occasional puffs of steam still popped from the radiator. Smoke signals.

'People are good about helping.' I meant, in this country. I meant unlike people in your country.

Chip missed the point. 'Yeah. Most people are kind enough.'

'So they'll pick you up. If you start walking one of those kind enough people will pick you up.'

'My pack's too heavy for walking.'

'So sit beside it and thumb.'

He stretched. 'I'm in no hurry.'

I went for a walk and practised saying, *Go away. You're not my problem. You're not getting back in that car.* Beneath the grass the ground was pitted from the early spring floods. No trees, not even a gorse bush where I could squat to pee. I kept looking around to see what Chip was doing. Did he see my speed, the anger that propelled me? Those driving past would think, with satisfaction, that we'd had a fight.

About then I remembered that it wasn't a hummingbird, that movie with Gregory Peck, but a mockingbird. My error felt grimly significant.

Between one backward glance and the next Chip had climbed into the driver's seat. How far would he get before the motor seized? I began walking backwards so I could watch. I was philosophical about this next link in the day's chain of events. The sun was now beating down and in the paddock across the road the lambs glowed so white as to seem phosphorescent.

There was a shattering blast of radio, which was quickly adjusted downwards. Greg had been exchanged for an over-excited DJ. I turned around again and walked until Phil's car was reduced to a Tonka toy and the DJ was no more than a wasp's intermittent buzzing.

There was a song on that Greg Brown tape about a woman with a 'slant six mind'. The words thrown in without explanation, as if slant six was an expression people used all the time.

'I've been so slant six this morning.'

'Yeah, me too.'

How come I hadn't heard of it?

As I was walking back Chip began to tip water into the radiator. It gasped and hurled the water straight back. Chip tried again. The same. Again he raised the container. 'I think it's too soon,' I called.

'Not too soon. It's coming right.'

He was a man and men knew these things. I watched while he poured in all the remaining water. 'It's keeping it down,' he said, like a new father. 'I think we'll be right.'

We peered into the metal throat. The water had disappeared. No sign of leakage, so it had to be in there. The needle on the gauge was still up past H. I pointed this out.

'Yeah,' said Chip. 'Not working. I'd say it never was.'

And so would I, now the thought had been planted.

'We'll be right now.' He screwed on the cap. He'd had enough of waiting. 'How far to the nearest gas station?'

I had no idea. The DJ was inviting his listeners to guess the colour of his pubic hair. I replaced him with Greg, and drove slowly, looking out for a signpost. The sunroof was open and our windows were down. Chip threw back his head and sang 'OooooOO, Oklahoma where the wind . . .'

He knew all the words: they'd done it at school and he was, like, Howard Keel. He sang with his mouth open so wide that, just glancing, you saw his epiglottis. It looked clitoral, which made me think rather warmly of Phil. Sex wasn't exactly his strong suit but there was enough there to miss.

Thinking of Phil led to thinking of what Phil wanted. Babies and stuff. Now, because of the radiator and everything, it seemed inevitable. He'd be seriously upset and I'd be wanting to cheer him up. And who was to say those kinds of decision were never the right ones?

At the service station two overalled men and Chip hung over the motor, staring and poking. They made sounds of lament, not for me but for the car.

I heard Chip say, 'It belongs to her boyfriend.' They poured in water and it piddled out again onto the concrete. Halfway up the radiator was a hole the size of a walnut.

'There's your problem,' they said.

They wouldn't hazard a guess as to the damage done. Most likely the head and also the gaskets. If I just took it around to the workshop . . .

The mechanic scratched his ear and said he couldn't tell until he had it apart. And today they were knocking off early but, if we were lucky, they might have time to look at it for us.

'For me,' I corrected, but my heart wasn't in it. I could very easily have cried. I asked if there was somewhere I could wait. I said it wasn't my car and I needed to get hold of the owner to see what he wanted.

Chip had gone back to the service station shop. I followed him to say he should take his pack out of the car. He said, hey, he was in no rush, and anyway deserting a damsel in distress was the last thing he'd do. I barely protested; at least he was a familiar face.

The public bar was the only one open. The bar staff — a man and a woman — were wearing satin. Crimson and scarlet, green and lemon. They could have been clowns or Spanish dancers — the cringe-making small-town version. A gimmick to bring in the tourists? If so, it wasn't working. Apart from me the only person in the bar was a tubby man in chequered red and brown trousers. He was setting up a portable organ. I asked him if there was a phone and he pointed me to it. It was in an alcove. The kind of phone that won't tell you the price until you've dialled the number. I went back to the bar to get an assortment of coins and Chip was there with a huge ice-cream running away on him.

I said, 'There might be a bus. Or a shuttle. If you ask.'

'Lou,' he said, 'what kind of a swine do you take me for?'

The kind who buys just one ice-cream. But what I said was, 'Suit yourself.'

The señorita changed my note for coins. I told her my car had broken down, hoping for sympathy, but none was offered. Around her armpits the satin was dark with perspiration.

I got through to the receptionist at Phil's school and asked her to take an urgent message. Instead she went off to look for him while I fed in coins and watched them devalue.

She returned. 'He's in class.'

I gave her the message. I said it was very important that he ring me at . . . 'This phone,' I shouted to the amigos. 'What's the number?'

Of course they didn't know. Had I looked on the side?

I looked on both sides. I looked underneath. I fed in more coins. 'Your number then? The hotel number?'

They appeared not to hear me. The man at the organ played some chords. 'One minute,' I shouted into the receiver and let it drop. I ran to the bar and searched for a phone. I ran back to the alcove mouthing the number in case it escaped me. Five seconds to spare. 'Hello, the number is 03 7865 990.' Or was it 7856 990? The call was cut off.

I returned to the bar for more coins. I got the señor to write the number down. The organist was playing 'Some Enchanted Evening'. Chip sang along as he fed the poker machine.

This time the phone at the school was engaged. Three more tries and I got through. The receptionist was terse.

The bar was filling up. I bought a lager and took it outside to the solitary plastic table. It was even hotter outside. The carpark was crowded with utes and 4WD wagons. Men with their sleeves rolled up — a few with women as well — hurried inside. You could tell they'd spruced up by the damp furrows in the hair and the fold marks in the jeans.

Soon the bar was packed, and this was a weekday afternoon. It appeared that the farming sector was doing rather better than it let on. In snatches, beneath the buzz and cackle, I could hear the organ playing 'The Happy Wanderer'. I wondered if Chip knew the words.

Had we stumbled into some local celebration — a birthday or farewell? The bar staff would be too busy to take Phil's call. They may not even hear it ring. Or they'd answer but not come looking.

I quickly drained my glass and stepped inside, easing my way between checked shirts and plaid shirts. A familiar face — the mechanic. He gave me a nod. He'd changed out of his overalls. He saw the question on my face and shook his head: not yet.

Beyond the organ going tralalee tralala was the sound of coins tumbling out of a poker machine. People craning to see, as they would for a car smash or a rugby try.

I reached the bar. 'Afternoon, love,' said the man on my right, making room. 'Enjoying yourself?' Above the bar counter the satin sleeves were flashing semaphores. I'd be waiting a while.

'Shaping up,' my new friend said — I thought he said — in a cheerful voice. He was looking past me, over to where the coins were still tumbling. He turned back. 'Where you from then?'

'Christchurch.'

'What, love?' he pressed closer. An ear tufted with ginger hair.

I shouted. 'Christchurch.'

The coins came to a halt.

'Passing through, are you?'

'Sort of.' I peered over the bar. The phone was still there.

He swung his refilled jug over my head without spilling a drop. 'See you again.'

'Just ginger ale,' I told the señor.

He upturned a glass. 'Who are you backing?'

'Sorry?'

'The cup.' He stabbed a thumb towards the screen set high in the corner. A jockey adjusting his stirrup, then back to the studio commentator, the one with the cleft chin. 'Fifteen minutes and they're off.'

The Melbourne Cup. But of course. He was not a señor but a pretend jockey and I was trapped in this bar with a horde of punters. Not that I'd have wanted to lay a bet. Something told me it wasn't my lucky day. When the organist graunched into 'Luck be a Lady' I knew it for sure.

As I reached for my glass I caught sight of Chip leaning across the other end of the bar, waving for my attention. We both leaned forward. 'Whadda y' know? I just won me two hundred and forty smackeroos. How 'bout that?'

I ground out a smile. Ever since I'd been in this place thoughts of money had been whining away in my brain. How much would a radiator cost? How much for a head? And a gasket, or rings and a valve grind? It may not be all my fault, but I would have to offer to pay at least half. What with?

Chip burrowed and shoved his way towards me.

'So what gives?' he demanded.

I must have looked blank.

'You and the slant six motor car — what's the story?'

'Slant six?'

'Joking,' he said.

'You know what it means?'

'It means . . . you know, grunty. I think you'd say souped up. So what's the story? We hitting the road or what?'

The race had started. Around us the crowd grew silent. Just the commentator doing his thing.

'I'm dealing with it,' I told Chip. 'I'm onto it. Soon as anything breaks I'll let you know.'

I patted him on the shoulder as if we were buddies. But inside me something — some intestinal equivalent of a bra strap — snapped. I actually felt it go ping, and then the relief. While everyone else, Chip included, was watching that high-slung screen, I walked out of the pub and up the empty street to the garage. I unlocked the boot of Phil's car and I dragged out the designer backpack with matching tent and bedroll. I sorted some food and a change of clothes and I gathered my tapes. Then I dredged in the glovebox for a pen and wrote a note on the back of an eftpos slip.

Dear Phil, it said. *I seem to be Protestant.*

WANTING

Lucia was always *wanting*.

Rob liked that word, the economy of it. One word, two meanings. And, in Lucia's case, since one sense was certainly applicable, the other became equally true.

Wanting and Lucia went hand in hand.

Some days Rob wrote secret lists of the things that Lucia had, over the years, needed in order to be happy. Inventories that were never completed because he'd try to be fair and fairness required so many decisions. Where, for instance, did necessity end and want begin? And should he count the small purchases? And, if so, where to draw the line? Was $40 an extravagance?

This would, surely, depend on whether the purchase was of any subsequent use or pleasure.

In his judgement, or Lucia's?

Which was the kind of question Rob's counsellor asked him.

Rob had found this, initially, dismaying. Having taken the rather drastic step of finding a counsellor, he was expecting more than someone who asked the very same questions Rob had for years been asking himself. Had Rob not been in the habit of asking himself those kinds of questions he would have had no reason to seek out a counsellor.

So — in Rob's judgement, or Lucia's? A ridiculous question since for Lucia every unnecessary purchase (amend that to every purchase of a non-essential item) brought at least a moment of pleasure. The very act of exchanging money or its digital substitute for the item or service in question made Lucia's saliva thicken, her heart beat faster.

At least that's how Rob imagined she felt. He'd tried asking Lucia but she'd always turn the question around. What was the matter with Rob? Money was for spending. It was normal to like shopping. Why was Rob so miserly? So small-minded?

Was he? He couldn't entirely dismiss the possibility.

'Not everyone's like you,' Lucia would point out.

Neither was everyone like Lucia. 'Not *everyone*,' Rob might have said, if he was her, 'loses all interest in an acquisition within days of its purchase, their sights already set on something else.'

If he was Lucia he wouldn't even be aware that the statement was grammatically incorrect.

He never remarked on the errors she made. In fact these days he barely noticed them. Grammatical errors were, it seemed, normal these days. Just like shopping. And Lucia hadn't had Rob's social and educational advantages. He took that into account; even had moments of envy. Given an underprivileged childhood, Rob's horizontal career path in middle management would have been an achievement.

All the same, he wouldn't have wanted Lucia's genes.

He didn't approve of those kinds of thoughts, the wider implications; yet they surfaced whenever he thought of his in-laws. Every one of them driven by irrational needs or unreasonable hopes.

Lucia and her family did not choose their gene pool. It was simply bad luck. Rob can see everyone's point of view. That's why he found a counsellor: it seemed like a way to narrow his vision. This was after Lucia had brought home the rug, every knot tied by the delicate coffee-coloured fingers of a child at the Aravalli Orphanage. There was a sketch of the orphanage on the accompanying leaflet — it looked like a log cabin in the Canadian mountains.

'See,' said Lucia, stroking the deep red pile, 'we've helped them survive.'

'Rubbish.' Rob tossed the leaflet aside. 'They'd be kids all right, working for slave wages in some hideous back-street sweatshop.'

He had no evidence that this was so, but it was only two weeks since the pool extensions had been completed and he was a little tense. He raised his voice. 'What is it with you?' he shouted. 'Buy, buy, buy.'

Lucia shrugged and smiled sweetly. 'I guess I'm just good at it.'

'You ought to be — you've had plenty of bloody practice.'

What he wanted to say was you couldn't be good or bad at shopping. Bartering, yes, if you lived in that kind of society. But bartering, anyway, would go against Lucia's absolute belief that the more a thing cost the greater its value. 'I'm ashamed,' she'd lie to her friends, 'at what we paid for it.' Then wait for them to demand the figure.

But Rob knew what Lucia meant when she claimed to be good at shopping. She was saying she had good taste. Those things she selected (for even Lucia couldn't buy all the stock in every shop she entered) were much coveted by her friends. Who also, naturally, had good taste, though not quite as good at Lucia's.

A philosophical discourse on the morality of shopping would

not have cut any ice with Lucia, but it would surely have prevented Rob's unprecedented and unrestrainable urge to slap her. Never before had he done such a thing. Clearly he was in need of help.

'I need her to change,' he told the counsellor.

She smiled gently. 'We can't make someone else change, Rob. We can only change ourselves.' Another little smile (oh, they were plentiful at the start). 'Perhaps we could consider the alternatives open to you?'

'That's the trouble,' he said stubbornly. 'There aren't any.'

The counsellor just sat there, her head on a lean as if this gave her a clearer perspective of her client.

Rob felt obliged to go on. 'I could leave her, of course. But I'd feel I was leaving because of money. No other reason. And that's not me — not how I want to think of myself.' He scanned her face for approval or sympathy but saw no emotion that he could identify with confidence.

'She's an addict,' he blurted. 'That's what it comes down to. For some people it's gambling, or cigarettes or drugs. With Lucia it's shopping.'

The counsellor's eyebrows twitched and Rob felt encouraged.

'Addicts can quit. They can be helped.'

At last the counsellor's smile returned with a gentle shake of the head.

'About you, remember. We were thinking about *your* alternatives.'

'There aren't any.' Rob's voice was harsh in his own ears. 'It's up to her.'

And he felt a kind of jubilation. At last he was facing up to reality, his decision made. 'Thank you,' he said, struggling up out of the reclining chair. 'Thank you, you've made me see —'

She raised a peremptory hand. '*Or*,' she said, 'or we could look at ways in which you might come to terms with the situation. '

Rob fell back, astounded. 'You mean, just accept?'

'People do. Many, many partners learn to do just that. In situations not unlike to your own.'

A revelation. Rob mulled it over during the week that preceded their next appointment. People agreeing to live in poverty and insecurity, in shame or fear because . . . because the alternative was even worse? Surely not. So — because they were simply unable to walk away. They lacked the courage — or cruelty — that the act of leaving demanded. They were the sort of people who were incapable of not looking back.

Rob sort of people.

'Would you leave her,' reasoned the counsellor, at their next session, 'if she was disabled in an accident or had a terminal illness?'

'Things she couldn't help?'

'Is it really so different?'

Yes, yes, yes.

'Maybe not,' Rob said, feigning an open mind.

Long ago, before Rob met and fell for Lucia, he'd spent his Saturdays searching junkyards and garage sales for gadgets and furniture that was broken or chipped or stained. He would take them home to repair, re-upholster, restore. It had given him great satisfaction.

'So you feel a need to improve things? What does that tell you about your relationships?'

This time the counsellor went to her desk and shuffled through files so that Rob could have time to consider. But he had the answer ready.

'That I want them to last.'

He knew it wasn't the response she was angling for, almost knew what her next words would be.

'But your need to *improve* things?'

Sometimes Rob suspected his counsellor wasn't actually on his side. Whenever he mentioned Lucia in connection with money or shopping (and after all, that was the reason, the only reason, he was here) the woman's eyes would narrow slightly and their focus slide past his shoulder to the window. A male counsellor might be more empathetic, but how could Rob change mid-stream without causing offence?

Lucia certainly treated people the way she did possessions. Her desire for him had been, at first, wonderfully obsessive. And though he hadn't, in the years that followed, been cast aside or replaced, Rob had become aware that her affection for him was closely related to his uncomplaining acceptance of their growing indebtedness.

Even their daughter Zoe, the most wanted baby in the universe, had become, within six months, little more than the reason why they must have a house full of velveteen giraffes, lions and teddy bears and interlocking kauri puzzles and designer mobiles and Pumpkin Patch catalogues and devices in which the baby could swing, rock, bounce, climb, travel or dance, should she feel inclined.

Lucia's heart had then set itself on becoming a clothes designer and she enrolled for a three-year course. Not for a moment did Rob think she would last the distance. It was he who got Zoe ready, each morning, for creche and dropped her off and picked her up and fed her crusts and read her stories and pinned up her drawings. (Unfairly, it was always Mummy that Zoe drew — bird's legs, big hair and a smile that stretched beyond her face.)

And, though she got fed up in the last year, Lucia stuck with the course and got her diploma. Which was a reminder of how wrong Rob could be.

Sometimes, Rob told his counsellor, he thought it was all a matter of projection. His negative thoughts about Lucia had a way of being proved right. Which could be just his own interpretation. Or could mean that he had power to influence Lucia's behaviour.

The counsellor gave an encouraging nod. Her face said *and*?

But Rob wanted an opinion. Was that possible? he prompted. Projection? Did she think . . . ?

His counsellor chewed at the end of her yellow ballpoint to indicate reflection.

'We see what we want to see,' she said eventually.

Rob took it that she was referring to him, to his suspect vision. He sat in silence, sulking.

'You were going to make a list,' she reminded.

'I did,' he said. 'I forgot to bring it.' The pros and cons of life with Lucia. He'd started on the cons, which were more easily defined but they made him depressed.

'So how did you feel about making the list?'

She was always asking how did he feel.

'A traitor,' he said. 'I felt like a traitor. We'd been having a good week. The commission she's got, it meant long hours.' No time or energy to even think about shopping.

'It seems she works hard.'

So did Rob work hard, but he knew that wasn't a good thing to say.

'She does,' he agreed in a voice of respect. 'Yes, she works hard.'

For little return. But he'd already made that clear. Deduct her expenses and the net profit was in fact pitiful. Lucia, however, refused to see it that way. Insisted on mistaking turnover for income and thus felt entitled to be extravagant. Rob had done the sums: they'd be better off if Lucia gave up the business — her licence to spend — and stayed at home. Except that boredom triggered her urge to shop.

'If she was an employee . . .' He had also said that before. He felt a stab of pity for his counsellor having to listen to words that went round and round like a drill, boring down. Boring.

'The ironic part is,' he said, 'that in the eyes of my employers Lucia is what we should all be like. In fact the assumption is that we are all like her. Always wanting new, different, more convenient, more stylish . . .'

Could he assume that his counsellor would, at least in this, be on his side? Vyella open-necked shirt, dark green trousers and jacket, cropped hair. Possibly butch but he'd been resisting that thought as irrelevant. Her lack of resemblance to Lucia had seemed in her favour.

'Maybe,' he tailed off limply, 'that's the way most people are. These days. Maybe it's me who is out of step.'

He was paying the woman. If reassurance was too much to ask at least she could offer a smile.

'It's like we're symbols of opposing forces.' Her silence still had a way of making him babble. 'Me and her. Consumption versus conservation. There's something more than debts at stake here.'

'What are you telling me, Rob?'

He sighed, looked down at his hands. 'I don't know.'

Her rooms were on the first floor. Her window offered a close-up view of thousands — possibly millions — of small heart-shaped leaves. A beech. Or was it a birch?

'I'd like to live in the bush, away from everything.' The certainty of it took him by surprise. ' It could be that it's the world — society — that I don't know how to handle. And Lucia somehow seems to represent that world. Like, she belongs but I don't.'

What a great job to have. Just sitting there. A few words now and then, like a spoon listlessly stirring. He should make this the last session.

Around about then he thought of another option. He would wait for Lucia to die. It wouldn't take forever — she was by nature incautious. He would simply cease to remind her about matters of safety.

That must be how they did it, all those long-suffering partners. What his counsellor took for acceptance and equanimity was the easier virtue of patience. A few, perhaps, were even driven secretly to help fate along.

Rob latched onto the concept of projection. Nervously, in idle moments, he would envisage fatal accidents, heart attacks, aneurisms. Nothing prolonged or unnecessarily painful. He was scared it might work, afraid it might not.

It didn't. Out of the blue Lucia announced that she had fallen in love with the young man who came to repair the electrical fittings in her showroom. Her half of the house could go to Zoe, and Rob must keep all their possessions. Lucia wanted a different kind of life. Her young man owned a hut and twenty-five hectares in the Hurunuis. A dirt track and no electricity (which, given his occupation, was a little ironic). A humble dwelling but more than enough for Lucia and her young man to be lyrically happy in.

'Cheer up,' Zoe told her father. 'She'll be back in three months at most.'

'My chance to escape,' Rob told the counsellor. 'I mustn't be there for her to come back to.'

They sat in silence.

'But if I'm *not* there,' Rob worried aloud, 'I won't know whether or not she came back looking.'

'Do you need to know that?' The counsellor was sounding a little bored.

'Of course I need to.' Having spent so much time in the counsellor's company Rob no longer felt obliged to hide his impatience. 'In order to understand why.'

'Why she came back?'

'No.'

'Why she left you?'

'No.' It was a kind of victory, having her do the talking.

'So, Rob, what is it you need to understand?'

Rob took a deep breath. He couldn't believe he was having to spell it out for her. 'I need to know what it was about me that drove her to shopping.'

His counsellor seemed to expand. Her even white teeth flashed Rob a smile and she clapped her hands.

'I'm proud of you, Rob. You're taking full responsibility for your own actions. This is a breakthrough, Rob. How does it make you feel?'

Rob smiled at his counsellor. How could he not? Despite his past suspicions, she cared about him, was on his side.

JEN'S ROOM

The room belongs to a woman called Jen. It's a small room, made even smaller by the floor-to-ceiling shelves that line one wall. These shelves are packed with yarn, raffia, lengths and scraps of material, small baskets full of needles, fastenings, scissors, and wooden gadgets the purpose of which Heather is unable to fathom.

Photos and postcards and pictures from magazines are pinned haphazardly over the remaining wall space. Heather has studied each of the photos but cannot decide if Jen is there. One of a group of beaming faces, or the thin woman dangling a hen by its legs? Perhaps the plump little girl in an alice band, with someone's hand intruding into the corner of the frame?

She must remember to ask Steph. Yet asking should be unnecessary. So much of Jen is in this room crowding in on Heather she ought, surely, to be able to identify her at a glance.

Heather treads carefully, lightly, in this room. Partly for fear that if she dislodges one small item she may be lost in a handcraft avalanche, but mainly because Jen's life is stored here and Heather feels like an intruder. Though Steph has assured her that unoccupied rooms in this house are frequently used by friends, and friends of friends. In which case, if Heather were Jen, she would have packed her possessions away or taken them with her.

The bed is — unsurprisingly — a futon: low to the floor yet comfortable. Heather has slept soundly in this bed and God knows she needed a decent sleep. For months she had only cat-napped. Either his snoring is worse or she has lost the facility for sleeping deeply.

Even in this matter she can't decide.

'It's inevitable,' he said. 'We grow, we change. Things change. But of course you are still dear to me. What more do you want after all these years?'

She thinks, too often, of the past. Sleeping under stars on high summer nights. Or not sleeping, because there wasn't the time — so much to say, so much to feel. The way his voice permeated her bones.

'What are you watching?' Placing herself in the doorway. Silly question — she could see the batsman, all padded up like an American baseball hero.

'Second all-dayer.' His eyes were fixed on the screen. The ball went wide. 'What about you?'

'The movie on Channel One. It's really quite good.'

'Time to think about what?'

'Whether there's any point in our staying together.'

That got his attention. One arm in his shirt, the other out and going nowhere. 'Is this some kind of joke? What do you mean, "any point"? We're fine. I think we're fine. Correction: I *thought* we were fine.'

She looked away, at the unmade bed. 'Maybe we are. Maybe I just need a break.'

'A break. Yes, well, maybe you do.'

'So when do you come back?'

'I don't know yet. I told you that.'

'But work . . .?'

'They owe me a week, but I might take some leave without pay. It depends.'

'Depends?'

'On . . . how I feel.'

'It's just the age you're at. Hormones. Would be a whole lot cheaper just to go to the doctor.'

'Yes, it would've been cheaper.'

'Shall I come in with you? In case there's been a delay.'

'No, don't worry.' The cricket would already have started.

'Okay, then. Love to Steph.' A peck on the side of her mouth, delivered warily, as if she was suddenly not to be trusted at close range.

He waved from the car. She watched until it was out of sight, just in case he came back, held out his arms and pleaded. She remembered a whole stretch of time when they tortured themselves with possibilities. If you die . . . If you left me . . . When you lose a leg you go on feeling the limb for ages after it's gone. That's what they say.

Steering her bag into Domestic Departures and Arrivals Heather imagined eating alone — sardines on toast — in a sunny kitchen with hollyhocks tapping on the window.

Steph, on the phone, and edgy. 'Just there's something I better tell you. I mean, it's not a secret or anything, only I didn't exactly spell it out because of Dad. Him freaking out is not what I need right now. Not what I need at all. Well, anyway, here goes: you know Charlie who I live with . . .'

'Charlie didn't come with me,' said Steph as she heaved Heather's suitcase onto the back seat of the stationwagon. 'She thought you might need some time to come to terms with it or whatever.'

Steph was wearing a long orange skirt, her disorderly hair clipped up. The skirt was blackened and wet at the hem and it clutched at her sandals.

Helen peered through greasy windows. 'A car seat?'

Steph grimaced. 'Don't worry, it's not our car. Ours doesn't have a warrant so bringing it into the city is not a good move.'

Steph flicked the belt across her chest but didn't bother to do it up.

'So do you?' she asked, navigating the maze of airport roadway. Rain hung in the air, water squishing beneath the tyres. 'Need to come to terms . . .'

'No,' said Heather. 'At least, I don't think so.'

Heather has met women who are privy to the nature and details of their daughters' sex lives. It makes her feel that she and Steph are estranged but they may both prefer it that way.

'I won't know that till I meet her, will I?' She threw Steph a grin and allowed herself, now, to buckle her daughter in.

'Did you tell Dad?'

'No.' Revisiting the wave from the car window before he drove off. Why hadn't she told him? It would at least have elicited some emotion.

She had a picture of Charlie in her head but wasn't aware of this until the real one turned out to be so different. At least a decade older than Steph, with a carpet of grey close-cropped hair, eyes that sloped down at the outer edges and a black homburg. Steph has since joked that Charlie even wears the hat to bed.

She was waiting for them at the café, at a table with friends. When Heather and Steph walked in the laughter stopped, caught in the air, and heads turned. Charlie got up and loped towards them. Floppy jeans belted tight at the waist, bare tanned feet, a leather jerkin over a faded blue shirt, and of course the hat.

Charlie has two children, ten and thirteen, who live with their father, but Heather reminds herself it is unfair to judge without knowing the whole story. Charlie moves and speaks with a confidence that makes Heather feel vaguely patronised, but that might be Heather's problem, not Charlie's. Truth is, it's the hat that bothers Heather most of all. She's still struggling to decipher the statement that it's surely making.

Four days now, and Charlie and Heather have rubbed along with only a hint of abrasion. Heather lies on Jen's bed awaiting sleep, and imagines the two of them up there in their house in the bush discussing her. She's been carefully vague about when she is leaving, but they will take it for granted her visit is finite and may already be counting the days.

No point in burdening Steph with her own indecision, that's what Heather's been thinking. Though there have been moments when the words were in her lungs battering for release. *What should I do? What would you do?* Remembering then that this is her youngest, her baby. To seek advice from your child on a matter that stretches back beyond her lifetime seems like an irrevocable act, an abdication of parenthood.

If you wait long enough a solution will present itself unbidden; that's what she's found in the past. Though the problems concerned were, surely, less fundamental, and anyway does she have time for long enough?

To her dismay Heather has found herself thumbing through the magazines stashed in a carton beside the fireplace, scanning advice columns and the probable fate of Leos. She does this even though the magazines are several years old.

One thing she knows for sure: this place is laying claim to her. She could live here. Not, perhaps, as Steph and Charlie do — lugging gas bottles and other essentials up the hill to a two-roomed shack perched in the bush — but in a proper house down here in the valley.

Or she could stay on in this house. Already she has become attached to its air of placid decay and the curious jumble of other people's possessions. There are only two bedrooms (she hasn't even peeked into the second room, taking the closed door as a perfectly reasonable plea for privacy) and both are currently claimed, though the occupants are elsewhere earning a living.

That is, of course, the drawback. What would she do by way of an income? Steph works in the café as a baker of rolls and croissants and pies. Just two mornings a week at this time of year, but five, sometimes six, in the holiday season. When she wrote to them, gleefully, about the job, Steph's father had grumbled about the waste of a good education.

Charlie, too, works in the holiday season, taking tourists on horse treks deep into the hills. The horses belong to the farmer who owns the paddocks on the flat below Charlie's home in the bush. Charlie is also one of the several owners of this house that Jen and Heather — and how many others? — have been glad to make use of. There are other homes, nestled like tree huts up in the bush. You wouldn't know they were there were it not for the tendrils of smoke drifting from wood stoves. Steph's taken Heather along sodden bush tracks to visit a couple of the closest neighbours. Inside the tiny houses the talk was as soothing as the rain that has fallen almost continually since Heather has been here.

Heather recognises this place from childhood as the world she'd built in her head. Now, as then, she is enchanted. Whether she stays or goes she will be warmed by the knowledge that such a place exists.

At whose expense? she imagines Steph's father saying. She tends to agree. She tries not to notice how often the talk here centres on the problems of getting and keeping the dole when work can be found elsewhere.

People drift in and out of this house, come to use the phone or the fridge or the washing machine, which sits on the back verandah in a shawl of jasmine. 'You must be Steph's mother,' they say, and their voices have a congratulatory ring. They are fond of Steph. Heather is glad to be Steph's mother.

They leave her alone, Steph and Charlie, just enough. At night she sits on the verandah watching the misty rain drift down. For someone teetering on the edge of major change she feels, most of the time, amazingly tranquil.

She delays ringing home. He'll want to know when she's coming back and she hasn't an answer. Telling him she hasn't yet made up her mind seems even worse than saying she's leaving him. Possibly she also wants to give him time to miss her; it's hard to be sure about these things.

She rings her boss and says she'll be taking a week of unpaid leave. The boss, having been forewarned, accepts the news without protest.

On the sixth day Heather rings home. She still hasn't made her decision but the call is Steph's idea and so can't be slid out of. And it's Steph who talks first and says to her father breezily, 'I'm not giving her up so soon. You'll just have to wait.' So when it's Heather's turn she simply says, smiling at Steph, 'You heard her. She won't let me go home so I'm taking another week.'

A grunt and then, 'I must say you're sounding more like yourself. I told you a break was all you needed.'

It's not a question; he doesn't require a reply. Heather asks how the cricket is going.

When she hangs up she turns to Steph. 'He's fast becoming a grumpy old man.'

'Mum,' says Steph, 'he always was.' She's grinning, but something must show in Heather's face, for the grin quickly dies and Steph heads for the kitchen, throwing words over her shoulder as she goes. 'But you're used to it, I know, so you take no notice.'

This is the moment for Steph to be told. Heather feels blood rush to her face and neck as she struggles to arrange the words in a suitable order.

Steph is filling the electric jug. 'It must be really good,' she says, her voice raised above the rush of the tap, 'to have reached that stage.'

'What stage?' Heather tugs at the neck of her sweater, inviting cool air.

'In a relationship. The stage, you know, when you can just accept someone for what they are, warts and all.' Steph flicks the jug switch and turns to Heather. 'Acceptance. I'm just hoping some day I'll get there. Devotion, you know. I can't wait to get past all this are-we-or-aren't-we-shit and just be calm and devoted.'

'Oh,' says Heather, and holds out her arms for Steph to step into.

'But it might never happen,' Steph mourns, an inch from Heather's ear.

Obligingly, Heather murmurs, 'Love, I'm sure it will.' She hears herself and is mortified. Releasing Steph she says in a bright voice, 'Which one is Jen? I've been wondering. All those photos. Come and show me.'

106

Jen is standing in front of a small but ornate Buddhist temple, competing. Her pin-striped trousers are almost hidden by a diaphanous orange shirt and on top of that she wears what appears to be a magician's cape, emblazoned with silver stars. Jen, too, wears a hat. It's the kind the Pope wears, soft and brimless. Her intense blue eyes stare defiantly out from beneath it.

Heather wishes she'd never asked.

FINAL DRAFT

Lately she's been finding his face in the oddest places. Tim Robbins wears his lips. Not, of course, the ones that she has glimpsed lurking, pinkly obscure, beneath white whiskers, but his lips as she knew them then. The haircut is now out of fashion, but still occasionally seen on Jeremy Irons. His eyes are in the possession of Johnny Depp.

She finds it so useful, this celebrity identikit.

'Who does this new one look like?' she asks her youngest grandson of his latest girlfriend.

He says, irritated, 'She looks like herself.'

His grandmother approves of this answer but grumbles anyway. 'Well, that's not much help to me.'

The grandson sighs. 'Okay. She looks a bit like Denise Richards.'

'Ah,' says his grandmother. 'Lovely.' She has never heard of Denise Richards.

Just a few days ago a shop assistant remarked on the grand-mother's resemblance to Katharine Hepburn. The grandmother was less than delighted; if she looked like a Hepburn she'd rather it was Audrey. She didn't say so. She was embarrassed by the discovery that, even now, she'd opt for prettiness.

When she was young she'd supposed that old people didn't mind the way they looked. Why would they, since there was no one they had to impress? When you were old (like, over thirty-two) your face became a description of the kind of person you were. Old faces, she had thought, were probably the only place in the world where people got what they deserved.

Every Monday she scans the movie ads, pretending she's not looking out for anything or anyone in particular. And on Tuesdays, in the matinee dark, she watches the workings of one man's mouth, catches a glance from the other's eyes and reassembles her first love.

Now and again she runs into him — the man he is now — at the central library. She would have passed him, that first time, without recognition if he hadn't spoken her name.

'Forty years,' he'd said. 'It must be, at least?'

Forty-four and a half, but she didn't correct him. His beard is a safety barrier between the present and the past. Sometimes she's wondered if perhaps he doesn't remember how it was with them, but of course he must.

They speak — she suddenly realises — in the slightly awed but mostly anxious fashion of those who have handed over all sense of responsibility for the way things are.

Alone in row G the grandmother is aware of luminescence. It could be the screen's reflection but she suspects it is her. For, certainly, she glows. As she did back then for him. But this time there is no rage or pain. No future, either. Nothing, this time, is at stake. This time it is, actually, *perfect*.

Between fiction shelves L and M he raises a fat-soled shoe. 'We had undue faith in leather,' he tells her. 'These days our shoes come inner-sprung. We walk on clouds.'

She laughs. 'We do. Indeed we do.'

It's amazing, she thinks, how things can turn out so well.

BIRTHSTONES

'Best to lie down.' Her mother's fat white hands press at Janine's shoulder. 'You need to be comfortable. A cushion.'

She snatches one — discoloured blue velvet with a sagging ruffle — from the arm of the sofa and holds it out. Janine gets a whiff of sour regurgitated milk, a smell that's becoming familiar and ridiculously appealing, making her heart skip in the way that everything about this boychild does. She had never imagined it could be like this — that he would have such power to enchant her.

She should have taken baby into their bedroom, closed the door, locked it if necessary. This is an intimate process. It would be scarcely more mortifying if her mother had suddenly taken it upon herself to instruct Janine in optimum positions for sex. 'This is how your father and I . . .' Janine's mind gags.

'I lay down with all three of you.' Her mother has collected more cushions, arranges them on the window seat beside Janine, who sees what is intended — the limp one for her neck, the plump beige one for her head, the blue one for the baby.

'Sitting like that you'll never get comfy, and he'll be taking in air, you don't want that. The important thing is to have you relaxed.'

Relaxed. Right. Grim laughter entrapped behind Janine's ribcage, curdling her milk. Her mother plans to stay for at least three weeks. At Steve's request. He arranged it before he left. Helen to fly down in time for the birth and stay through those first anxious weeks. And Janine, lumbering and fearful, had readily agreed. She must have someone with her and if it couldn't be Steve, her mother would do. Her mother, at least, knew about babies. This was the thinking of the other, pre-baby, Janine, who knew no better.

These last few days Janine has thought quite often of Tracey, though they haven't seen each other in years. Haven't even kept in touch. Janine and Tracey were best friends right up until, at fourteen, Tracey went, with her limping mother, to the tent of the healer who'd been on TV. It did nothing for Tracey's mother who remained lopsided, but a glowing finger reached towards Tracey and touched her just above the bridge of her nose, and from that moment Tracey was no longer the Tracey Janine had known. Nor could Tracey adequately explain to her friend the cause of her transformation.

It was more, she said, than the touch of that finger, which she couldn't exactly recall. At least not how it felt or whether it was hot or cold. She had, Tracey said with reluctance, been *spoken* to, though there were no words, there was no voice. There was no way to explain it — it was a *spiritual* thing. She'd heard it as if her heart had ears. And what Tracey had learned — the wordless, soundless message imparted by the finger — was that she belonged to Jesus.

This much Janine had learned only by pestering Tracey, who would intermittently wail *I know it sounds dumb* or *I don't expect you to understand.* Only if the same thing happened to Janine, said Tracey, would she ever truly comprehend.

But the healer had, by then, moved on, and Janine wasn't sure that in her heart she wanted to belong to Jesus. She could sense Him there whenever she and Tracey were together, and that was upsetting enough. He was with Tracey and three was a crowd. Suddenly she and Tracey seemed to have nothing much in common.

Now, almost ten years later, Janine thinks of Tracey and believes she understands. For Janine, too, has been, by one single event, transformed. Claimed, not by Jesus, but by Anton. The moment they placed the baby in her arms something momentous and irrevocable — something spiritual — happened to her. Is that how it is with motherhood?

All mothers?

'Raise your shoulder,' instructs Helen, Janine having obediently lowered herself and the baby onto the cushions. 'Perhaps move his wee head a tiny bit higher. Those breasts look almost empty to me. They did feed you properly up there? I had so much milk, especially with you, it just flowed and flowed.'

Janine doesn't wish for this mental image of Helen's weighty boobs spurting like shower nozzles, her own infant mouth nuzzling to clamp . . . Her stomach gives a threatening shudder and she does her best to push her mother out of the picture and concentrate on the fine soft hair on her baby's head, the vulnerable groove of the fontanelle. Imagines it large, like the indent where a spaceship has rested.

'You were such good babies.' Helen's voice is suddenly soft and wistful. 'So sweet. Adorable. I wished you could have stayed babies forever.'

Three of them, none more than two years apart. Janine in the middle. Their father left before Natalie had learned to walk.

Perhaps Helen has had the same thought: her voice is back to normal. Even the trace of amusement at Janine's expense.

'You're holding him like a teacup. He's flesh and blood, not bone china.'

'Because,' grits Janine, 'this is uncomfortable. It was better the way we were.'

'Cross-legged!' She makes it sound like *laggard.* A failing. 'The fastest way to ruin your back.'

Anton is making soft kissing sounds. His mouth, opening wider than her nipple requires, could be the mouth of a dying goldfish. Janine feels a wave of panic. Not the first, although in the reassuring bustle of the hospital they'd subsided quickly. Even here they are not rational, she must get used to them. But he is so tiny, so inexperienced at breathing, who is to say he will not suddenly forget how it is done?

'He's taking in air,' says Helen. 'He'll get a tummy ache. Try him on your other side.'

They said that at the hospital. *That side. The other side. The left one. The right one.* As if her breasts were separate entities competing with each other. As if there was a prize for productivity.

As Janine heaves them both off the cushions, Anton screws his face into a semblance of a tightly squeezed blood-red dishrag and screams. The noise is a bandsaw slicing into Janine's flesh. Her baby's rage is immense and personal; his clenched face is ugly and full of menace.

She presses him to her so that the volume is muffled. She's aware that if she increased the pressure by another notch Anton could be hushed forever. This is a thought she has not had before. Steve must never know of it. It wouldn't have come if he was here, surely it wouldn't.

When he gets back . . . and he will, she must stop thinking of it as a war. He told her that often enough — it is peace he's there for, the keeping of peace. A policeman more than a soldier, that's what he said. The old-fashioned bobby kind of cop, where *being seen* was what counted. They would be a *presence*, that's all.

In a land where the two sides look alike and neither speaks English. A conspicuously foreign presence in military uniform.

He shouted his unit when Anton was born. A bunch of Kiwi soldiers sculling beer on her baby's behalf. Men in a war zone, talking the jargon of war and secretly hoping for a skirmish or two before their term of duty is up. Wanting that experience: the fear, pain, adrenaline, self-knowledge . . . whatever it takes to convince a man that he is, indeed, a man.

When he gets back will he notice at once that she is an entirely different person? Will he too have changed? And will their respective changes hold them apart? Anton in the centre like a hinge from which each swings away from the other?

Four times Janine has written to her father and got no reply. The last time she'd told him she was pregnant. This morning, on their way home from the hospital, she told her mother about those letters. Helen had shrugged her bulky shoulders and said that was much as she would've expected.

Janine's father is, these days, a yachtsman who makes dangerous solo journeys across untravelled stretches of water. Janine's letters were addressed c/- the newspapers or (the last letter) a TV station that had interviewed him. She can't believe that none of those letters have reached him.

She wouldn't mind if he drowned.

Helen has removed the cushions and stacked them at the other end of the windowseat. Janine can't find the energy it takes to object — this is her mother. She's lifted the baby until his cheek is against her own. There he makes quavering heartbreak sounds in her ear.

In the hospital she picked him up whenever he cried and offered him, indiscriminately, a right or left tit, which he drank from or rejected. In the hospital her milk flowed boundless as love and the nurses, after that first supervised feeding, glanced and smiled and went on their way.

The baby had come ten days early — her second night alone in the queen size bed, and four days before Helen was due to arrive. Janine was amazed by her own calm efficiency. She packed her bag, rang the hospital, timed her contractions by the digital numbers on the VCR, ordered a taxi (no long-term parking at the hospital) and left dry food for the cat. She could have rung Sandi who would cheerfully have rushed to help, but Janine was happy, now the time had come, to do this thing alone. Or not really alone, for the baby already had a name and gender and could scarcely be discounted. He was, like his father, a presence.

Janine thought Helen's voice sounded relieved. That mother and child were fine, or because she'd not had to play a role in the birth? They agreed that Helen should stick with the arrangements she'd made and arrive in time to bring her first grandchild home.

Obediently Janine now eases herself and the baby onto the rearranged cushions. Tomorrow, after work, Sandi and Lowella are coming to see the baby. They wanted to come today but Helen said Janine would not be 'up to' a visit.

Janine is eager to see her workmates, imagines them at this moment giving lip to the grease-smeared men in the workshop. The pre-birth, unknowing Janine had arranged for six weeks' leave. Four plastic bottles with teats stand in the kitchen cupboard and the creche has been booked.

She wonders now why her plans weren't questioned by Sandi, who has nine-year-old twins. Because it is, of course, out of the question. In six weeks, in six months, even six years Janine will not be ready to wrench herself away from Anton. No one else in the world could possibly feel for this baby the way she does. He and she are attuned, they are intertwined.

He has now lost all interest in feeding, moves his head away from her nipple, miniature lips doggedly compressed.

Okay, so you've had enough. But the words stay in her head because her mother is there waiting to be consulted. 'He's not hungry,' she tells Helen, pulling her bra up to cover her breasts (left one and right one), happy that the ordeal is over. 'I'll feed him later.'

'What? In half an hour? Or less? Start down that track, missie, and you'll wear yourself ragged. He's hungry all right, but nothing will flow when you're so tense. You are. I can tell.'

A black rage fills Janine. Thick as fog. The baby's face is again tightening for a scream. Four days old and already he knows she is not and never will be the mother he hoped for and deserved. They're two of a kind, Anton and Helen. Janine pushes herself up straight and thrusts the screaming thing in the soft, soft cuddly-rug at her mother. Hears her own voice, shrill and crazy. 'You feed him then. You know all about it so you bloody feed him.'

On the bed she shares with the soldier when he's not away learning to be a man, she curls up and cries. When Janine had found her first boyfriend she'd dared to ask Helen why their father had left them. Some men, Helen had said, can't stand not to be the centre of attention.

Through the thin walls she can hear her mother talking to Anton in a high, foolish, goo goo voice.

SATAN.COM

There was this man who, in the eyes of the world and in his own eyes, was strong. His strength was not the steel-bending kind; it lay in the way he used words. Once, years before, when he'd been stranded in a small German village waving his hands and whimpering *Guten Morgen* and *Ich spreche nur English* until his wife arrived to rescue him, she had told him, 'You are like that Samson, only it is not the hair but the words. Someone slice off your English and you be poor weak man.'

His wife would often bemoan the inadequacy of her own English, but he had loved the way she used the language. It was as if she had scooped all the words into a container, shaken them about, and then tipped them out to fall into fresh and astonishing sequences. (In addition to German, his wife also spoke French and conversational Japanese but he had no way of knowing whether she used these languages in a more conventional way.)

They had visited the German village during his four months as a Writing Fellow in Berlin. It was his first and only visit to Europe and the last time they had travelled together. He found it ironic that his being a writer had enabled them to visit her homeland, yet was also the reason she died.

'No, no,' his friends would object, should he be misguided enough to voice this thought out loud. 'That isn't true. You can't blame yourself.'

But it was and he did.

If he had stayed in public relations, selling sincerity, hope and convector heaters, his wife would not have hung around like an apple with rot already spreading. Her life was the price of his literary career.

He wasn't to know. His friends would say that too. His friends had offices and salary packages and could well have said, *Well, you chose to be poor*, but they didn't — at least not to his face. Instead they said, *It's a national disgrace. Do you know what they pay Jonah Lomu? This is a nation of philistines.*

They were, after all, his friends.

But he was not, as they would suggest, a victim of circumstances. He knew how it was and he made a choice. Two novels and a cupful of praise was all it took to persuade him that he was entitled to the self-indulgence of what he thought of as a 'writing life'.

His wife had been in favour, but then she loved him and so put his happiness before her own. He was aware of this, and had tacitly approved, for he also put his happiness before hers. (Though at the time he thought of it not as happiness but, more portentously, as his soul or his sanity.)

It was a gamble. They had joked about fame and wealth and whether or not *popular* necessarily meant second rate. (Nowadays, that is. Not in Shakespeare's time, or Dickens', when lack of alternatives forged a higher standard of public appreciation.)

They did not speak of power, though in retrospect he could see that it was a major factor. As far back as he can remember this man had been aware of the power that lay in the skilful wielding of words.

He had learnt to speak before his brother, who was fifteen months his senior. The brother, a hefty child, had controlled his sibling by virtue of bulk and discretely administered biffs, but this balance of power was reversed when the younger brother was able to question, to taunt and tell on.

The younger brother thought he could remember the exact moment of realisation that things had changed, although at the time he was barely two years old. The memory he had was of his mother's frown and the fact that it enabled him to read her mind. Instead of being proud of her younger son, she was concerned that he was outstripping his older brother in a crucial skill. Up until that moment the mother had done her best to protect her younger son from his brother, but now (her frown said) it would have to be the other way around, and that would be much, much harder.

The boys' parents were socialists, even though this was already out of date. They believed in fairness and helping the underdog, so their younger son always felt slightly ashamed of his cleverness. It seemed reasonable that his brother should be roundly praised for getting a job on the assembly line at PDL, yet his receiving a university scholarship and straight A passes went almost unmentioned. He was aware that a soupçon of knowledge could be spun into a dazzling and apparently erudite discourse that was almost indistinguishable from wisdom. And he knew that his brother's head was chock-full of accurate facts, figures and formulae for which the brother got no credit on account of being unable to convey this information in a lucid fashion.

Despite his high grades the younger brother lasted barely two years at university. His sense of being advantaged weighed on him, and besides, he had begun to write a novel, and in New Zealand Lit. the urge to shout, *And me! Let's study me!* was almost overwhelming.

This same urge saw him regularly contributing poems, theatre reviews and outrageous lies, under three different pseudonyms, to the student magazine. When each of these personas had established a following he interviewed himself and — under a fourth name — wrote an admiring piece about his deception and versatility.

His wife-to-be used to turn up at the editorial office offering very ordinary photos of possums and ragwort and old man's beard which, because of her elfish good looks and charming accent, the editor would promise to use in some future issue.

On the strength of his journalistic initiative the student was offered a copywriting job with an up-and-coming ad agency. The pay wasn't great but there were regular increments and the work was unbelievably easy. At night he got on with his novel.

The editor of the student magazine received a pile of letters asking what had become of their favourite contributor. He suggested to the nubile young woman who took talent-free photographs that she might try her hand at reporting.

She arrived at the writer's student flat with her notepad and camera. He asked her what she was studying and she told him biology.

'So what's with the photo-journalism?'

'I want to meet people,' she said. 'Other people, you understand? Biologists not much having good fun.'

Four months later they left their shared flats and rented a place together, although for over a year she allowed her parents to suppose that her flatmate was a girl.

She graduated, but there were no jobs waiting for a freshly minted biologist — not unless she moved to another city, and, since he didn't want to leave, neither did she. He was earning enough for both of them to live in a careful fashion. She took a secretarial course — they lived in the capital city and secretaries were always in demand. 'It's fine,' she said. 'Biology, it was just a ticket not a vacation.'

'Vocation.'

He finished the novel and sent it off to a local publisher who said yes please. It was as easy as that. Eight months later the publishing editor flew down to give the writer his six free copies and take them both out to dinner. The book — two thousand, five hundred copies — had been printed and badly bound offshore and the reviewers made rather a lot of the way pages fell out, but they found the writing 'fresh' and 'humorous' and even 'lyrical'.

Despite their approval, sales figures were disappointing. But so what — he was a critically acclaimed novelist! And, as such, was headhunted to write speeches for a lazy but likeable opposition MP.

With a little coaching in presentation and timing the MP gained a reputation as a feisty man of the people who was, moreover, a bit of a wit. Two years later the MP became a Cabinet Minister in a newly elected left-wing government that very quickly changed its mind about whose side it was on. The speechwriter found it harder and harder to draft passionate speeches, let alone think up ministerial *bon mots*, but his ever-increasing salary gave reassurance that he was valued and upwardly mobile. He reined in his growing cynicism and poured his heart into his new novel.

This time the binding was perfect and the book was properly launched with speeches and finger food and wine. Just hours before the launch the speech writer/novelist and the secretary (who was now no longer a secretary but a *personal assistant*) were quietly but joyfully married on the balcony of their Oriental Parade apartment. His parents were there, as was her frail and recently widowed mother. His brother was best man. It wasn't a dressed-up kind of wedding but they'd bought the brother a suit so he wouldn't feel out of place. He had been laid off three years before and still hadn't found another job.

The second novel was a great success. The reviewers (all, that is, except Celestina Carruthers in the *Stratford Tribune*) were full of praise. *Runaway bestseller* boasted the diagonal yellow strip on the third local edition. Offshore interest was expressed.

The author, in a surge of over-excitement, told the Minister where he might, if inclined, put the speech writing job.

For a runaway bestseller the book made very little money. But it took the author a couple of years to realise that there was no pile of dollars temporarily jammed in the copyright pipeline. And by then a third novel was well under way.

His wife was willing to support them both, though this wasn't what either of them had envisaged. It meant a definite change of lifestyle. They no longer, for one thing, had friends around to dinner. Not even on impulse. Not even if someone called by when a meal was cooking (though she made an exception for his brother, whom she was fond of and felt sorry for).

His wife made all such decisions — her husband began to notice — without consultation. As if his opinions were no longer of any consequence. Though he, too, felt sorry for his brother, whose life seemed to be a continuous battle against the capricious and irrational decisions of government agencies. Each time, after an exhausting and totally fruitless exchange, the older brother would turn up on his sibling's doorstep with a sheaf of official and contradictory statements and demands, and the younger brother would compose highly civilised letters to commissioners and ministers on his older brother's behalf. *I am mystified* . . . he would write politely, or *I note with bemusement the somewhat startling logic* . . .

It worked every time.

He was correcting the proofs of his third book when his wife told him she was pregnant. 'Don't worry,' she said, ruffling his hair. 'We'll manage.'

But how could he not worry? From that moment on he began to say yes to all the time-consuming requests he had been turning down in order to have uninterrupted time to write. As long as the organisers would pay him *something*, the writer would agree to do whatever they asked. They wanted his services because he was a 'bestselling author', which they took to mean successful and famous.

He was a bear on a chain, dancing for coins.

He became hot property on the after-dinner speaker circuit. This wasn't much different from the job he'd had before, except that he had to be better dressed and the words came out of his own mouth instead of somebody else's. He still had to censor out anything that actually seemed worth saying, and he still had to make his audience laugh. He had very little time left for what he thought of as his 'real writing'.

On the advice of his publisher he applied for a literary grant to last one year (or approximately one-third of a book, since three years was how long it had taken him to write the last one). Because there were many applications for a very modest amount of money, he was awarded only a quarter of what he had asked for. (That is, he was given enough to write one twelfth of a book, or approximately one and a half chapters.)

When that money ran out he tried to get back on the after-dinner speaking circuit but was no longer in demand.

Their daughter weighed in at seven pound four ounces and, in the classified columns of the paper that carried her birth notice, the writer saw that his old agency was looking for a Creativity Executive with Writing Experience.

'Three novels?' said the personnel manager, looking up from the writer's CV. ' But are they any good? That's the question.

'I'll tell my kids I shook the hand of a real live author,' said the personnel manager, seeing the author out. 'Daughter's at varsity, bit of a bookworm. Bound to have heard of you.'

He looked not a day over twenty-three.

'What a cretin,' said the writer's friends. 'You're famous. You're in *Who's Who?*. You're a national treasure.'

When their child was six months old her mother rejoined the work-force. The work she did was the same as before but this time she was not a personal assistant but an administrator. Her husband, as the at-home parent, became (though the word never, ever, passed his lips) a caregiver.

He had intended to write in his spare time but discovered that, when he managed to find some, he was much too tired.

They got rid of their apartment on the Parade and the monthly ransom that was their mortgage, and bought a place in Tawa. His wife took the train to work each day, his daughter started school, and the man went back to being a writer.

His brother's luck, by now, had changed. He had a job working with computers. He was solvent and busy and no longer dropped in just before dinnertime.

There was no money for the daughter to go with her French class to Noumea, nor did she get the pony she so fervently wished for. Once in a while her father would come along to her school to talk to the senior students about his work. On these occasions his daughter would pretend she didn't know him.

The brother, meanwhile, had been promoted and then promoted again. He talked the talk, but his walk stayed the way it had always been: small steps and thighs that pressed together. He laughed at the sight of his younger brother tapping at the keyboard of a seventeen-year-old computer. 'Give it to the museum,' he said. 'If your equipment is obsolete what does that say about you? Get with it, upgrade, download, set up a website . . .'

But the writer was fond of his old computer. Together they had, by then, written three novels, a short story collection, four radio plays and a stage play. His novels had all been shortlisted for literary prizes and one had won but none had earned him decent money.

The daughter took out a large student loan and went off to study dentistry, that being the most pragmatic and lucrative profession she could think of. The year she left home her father was invited to be a Writing Fellow in Berlin. The fellowship was intended for a solitary writer, but he took his wife. They were accustomed to living simply and cheaply and, for the first time in twenty years, he had the chance to be the partner who paid the bills.

The following winter his wife had a heart attack, small but unnerving, like a hurled stone that had grazed her cheek. No real harm done, except for the knowledge that fate had it in for her and its aim would surely improve. Time to take evasive action. But the couple had decided some time before that their daughter, with her burden of debt, was the one who needed the health insurance, and the public hospitals were full of people higher on fate's list.

After her mother died the daughter hardly ever came home. 'I can find you on the library shelves,' she said, 'any old time I want to.' He took this to be an accusation, and didn't doubt that it was justified.

Writing had been responsible for the loss of his wife and the distrust of his daughter, but he continued to do it because it was what he knew. He'd long been aware of a widespread belief that writers should live alone, and now he understood why. This way they harmed no one else.

His daughter completed her studies and went travelling. She left him her email address. Every few days, she explained, she would call into an Internet café and read her mail.

In almost any part of the world this was now possible. To her father the words were like a blazing, blinding sun that you raise an arm to ward off.

'Send your manuscript as an attachment,' said the letter from the commissioning editor of the *Fictional Fathers* anthology.

'Are you aware that you are our only remaining author to still rely on fax or the mailman?' wrote his publishing editor with discernible irritation.

The writer tracked his brother down to a Cook Islands beach. A working holiday — just him, his laptop and a pina colada. 'I've looked in the shops,' he wailed, 'and I don't have that kind of money.' A memory of his brother gobbling down food at their dining table in Oriental Parade flashed into his head.

'Get a second hand PC,' said his brother. 'People upgrade and they almost give their old ones away. You want it to have a modem and Windows 95 or later.'

'Hang on while I write this down.'

There were twelve PCs for sale in the latest *Trade and Exchange*. The first two had already gone. He drove along a coastal road to find the third.

'See,' said the vendor. 'Greeting cards, sympathy if someone's died. Get your photos displayed on screen and Bob's your uncle. Very latest from Microsoft and all this stays on your hard drive.' He polished the screen with his sleeve to remove a couple of greasy streaks. The bedsit smelt like the inside of a well-trod gumboot.

'Spreadsheets . . . profit and loss . . . files . . . download . . . megabytes . . .'

'I work on a Mac,' interrupted the writer. 'I'll need to transfer manuscripts from that machine to this.'

'No worries,' beamed the vendor. 'The days of either/or are gone.'

At home the writer wiped the PC clean of dust and grease, set it up and had a go. It was like his Mac and it wasn't. Everything was back to front or inside out. Within minutes he was feeling like an elderly Alice in Wonderland: things kept happening but nothing made sense. Irrational options were offered to him in a nonsensical language. He told himself it was just a matter of time.

A week passed, and then another. The writer was still trying to transfer his work-in-progress from one machine to another. His brother was still away, so he had called on friends for help and advice. One by one they'd arrived, cheerfully brimming with tales of computer conundrums and glitches they had personally encountered, wrestled with and solved.

One by one these friends sat at the keyboard left-clicking and right-clicking. They selected, highlighted, inserted, searched and formatted with increasing frustration. Eventually (the writer came to know) they would say: *I'm not sure why it's doing that.* Or: *I've never struck that before.* And: *You may have to call in an expert.*

The writer rang around to see what an expert would cost him. Eighty dollars an hour. The writer looked up his earnings for the last financial year and did the calculations. His hourly earnings, averaged out, came to $2.81.

But, thanks to his friends he had made some headway. The work-in-progress had been transferred from his technologically-obsolete-but-functionally-perfect Macintosh to the hard drive of his technologically-acceptable-but-obstinately-non-functional IBM clone.

It had not, however, made the transition in a form that was recognisable to any of the twenty-five people (including two experts) to whom it was subsequently shown. Nor could they suggest any way of translating it.

And unfortunately the writer, in an effusion of gratitude to the friend who had finally managed to effect the transfer, had donated his Mac to this friend. Who, on reaching home, had dismantled it in order to mess with the electronic components.

Fortunately, the writer did have a copy on disk. He was able to get this document printed off so that he could retype a copy into his PC. He decided to let the matter of email wait until he had something ready to transmit.

The morning he began the retyping (one hundred and seventy-one pages of a first-draft novel) the writer advised his PC that he wished to create a new document. The PC was in the act of doing what it was told when a paper clip with bulbous eyes cruised onto the screen. It rode in on a lined A4 page semi-disguised as a magic carpet, and began to direct operations.

The writer did not wish for the company of an animated paper-clip. Searching the Microsoft Word menu for the means of its removal, he learned that the thing was his 'office assistant'.

The writer did not require an office assistant, but if he had wanted one it would not have been this one. For one thing, the creature was extremely unattractive. The writer had actual paperclips in his desk drawer and their appearance was quite pleasing, but this mobile version on his screen was ugly. Furthermore, its demeanour was mannered and coyly posturing like some pathetic old queen.

A pathetic *pissed* old queen who, beneath the artifice, was full of hostility and cunning and refused to be removed. Hiding the thing was the only option offered, and over and over the writer selected and clicked and the creature slid away in a camp and obsequious fashion. Then, within minutes, it would sneak back, blinking and simpering, and the writer would feel a gust of guilt. Was his dislike of the creature evidence of a burgeoning intolerance? Or (worse) homophobia?

So the writer dragged the office assistant to a corner of the screen and left it there in the hope that it could be ignored. He was still under the impression that he was in charge of proceedings. It seemed logical to suppose that, as the *writer*, he would decide what form the writing would take. It was, therefore, a considerable shock to discover that the self-appointed assistant considered itself authorised to instruct, correct and over-ride.

Here was a man whose job — nay, his *raison d'être* — lay in the selection, placement and presentation of words. In this he was an expert, a highly skilled craftsman. Yet this transsexual paperclip had the cheek, the temerity and the stupidity to dictate matters of sentence structure, grammar and layout.

Just as there is only one way of adding or multiplying figures, there is only one correct way of writing words. That's what the 'office assistant' was telling the writer, and it threw him into a state of rage that felt close to despair.

'Nazi,' he typed in the assistant's dialogue box. 'Philistine.'

Was this normal or had he landed a rogue computer? Had its components been tampered with, and if so was it deliberate? And in that case why him?

Was there a conspiracy?

Political or extra-terrestrial?

Whatever the intent, it had surely succeeded — he was a writer without words.

A carver with no hands.

A blind artist.

He rang his brother. 'This computer's no use to me. It won't do what I tell it. It doesn't even make sense.'

His brother laughed. 'Nothing makes sense. It's the way of the world. If that bothers you, take it up with Billy Gates.'

For the first time since he was one year and eleven months and seventeen days old the writer began to think of his brother as someone he had reason to fear. His brother and the paperclip had much in common: beyond the world of computer software neither had value or significance. So of course they were on the same side, and it wasn't the side the writer was on. This would seem to make them the enemy. And an enemy who has gone from powerlessness to all-powerful is an enemy to be feared.

Fear made the writer behave in a childish fashion. *Go fuck yourself, android worm*, he typed. The paperclip raised its eyebrows, shrugged and replied. *What would you like to do? Troubleshoot toolbars and menu . . .*

The next day the writer tried again — what else could he do? And now the paperclip took its revenge. Each time the writer opened the manuscript that was to be his intended novel, an accusing sign would appear on screen.

This computer has committed an illegal act and will now shut down.

And shut down it did. So, each time, the writer would have to push Reset and start again, but no sooner would he begin to type than the sign would reappear. *This computer has committed . . .*

That night as the writer lay wide awake wrestling with conspiracy theories he had a profound flash of insight. The office assistant was Satan/Beelzebub/Mephistopheles.

It made absolute sense. Never before had history offered the Prince of Darkness such a red-hot marketing opportunity. He'd have been crazy to pass it up. Windows (literally) into the minds and hearts of mankind. (Well, only the technologically advanced sector, but they're the ones who matter, since the future is in their hands. And, happily for Satan, they would also be the most receptive to his message, their spiritual fields having lain fallow, so to speak, for many years.)

If the writer was in the Devil's shoes and bent on global take over, the first thing he'd deal to was freedom of speech. And how better to do that than by controlling the order and presentation of written words?

Lying in the dark, the writer reasoned that Satan's manifestation as a transvestite paperclip must have been conceived and strategically planned over many, many years. Perhaps from the time Hitler had begun to look like a bad bet.

The writer wondered if he was the only person to have figured all this out. He was aware that this was the kind of information you could probably find on the Internet. If or when he finally managed to get his computer on-line it would be worth doing a search. Under *Satan*? *The Antichrist*? *Microsoft Office Assistant*?

But of course the Devil would have thought of that. The Internet as his domain — a satanic propaganda highway. With or without the complicit approval of W. Gates? Billy and Beezle — a deal struck?

The writer slid out of bed and went to the laundry cupboard where he kept the tools he needed for small repair jobs around the house. He selected the hammer and took it to his office. He switched on the computer and left-clicked on the mouse until the office assistant came sliding into hammer range.

Along with the shower of glass there were sparks and acrid smoke. The writer took this as confirmation of all he had feared. He returned to bed and eventually fell into a fitful sleep, littered with dreams.

In the last of these dreams his wife had returned and was in the kitchen making a cup of tea. At this point the writer woke and his ears affirmed the truth of his dream. He was, for a moment, wildly happy, but then reason took over and he laid a hand to his forehead. It felt feverish, as one might expect when one has just banished the Devil from his temple.

But the kitchen sounds continued, so eventually, and with puzzlement rather than trepidation, the writer got up and went to check them out.

The paperclip was sitting at his kitchen table, removing a tea bag from a mug the writer's daughter had given him for Father's Day when she was eleven. The creature had an elbow propped on the table, while the rest of its body drooped in a floppy Pink Panther fashion. The writer stood in the doorway wearing a pale green nightshirt. He observed the self-mocking attempt at elegance by a creature who was, in truth, grotesque. The writer noted the implicit pathos of this posturing and, despite himself, was moved by it.

The paperclip turned to gaze at him out of those bulbous eyes. The look it sent him was unmistakably feminine. The creature raised her brows. 'What would you like to do?' she asked, then blinked furiously. 'A cup of tea? Go back to bed? Write a bestseller?'

Her voice was softly familiar. Just a trace of accent remained.

LAMBS

He's aware of her striding from kitchen to passage: busy busy, angry angry. Her glare pierces the back of the sofa to lodge in the cranial space where his conscience should be.

The rain has changed direction. It batters, now, at the small side windows. The rain is on Andrew's side, absolving him, enhancing the glow of the one-bar heater that may be a factor in her fast-footed anger. The woodburner — an ugly seventies model set smackdab in the thoroughfare section of this all-purpose room — was his mother's doing, as was the open-plan 'family area'. She used to boast about the heat the burner 'threw out' and how one log of wood would burn for a week. Truth was, she never sat down long enough to know how cold it got down the TV end of the room.

In some ways the women have turned out to be alike.

And, just like his mum, she's been baking. Something cheesy — muffins or maybe a quiche. Too early for dinner so it might be for the freezer — something for him to heat up while she's in the hospital.

He could tell her it smells good but she'd think he was sucking up. He should've gone down the road to Roger and Jan's, told her he'd promised Roger he'd take a look at the bike, something like that. Down there they'd have a proper fire going and a carton of stubbies and maybe some of those honey-roast peanuts. Jan loves her rugby, curses and shouts like a man, and why not?

Trouble is, Jan would ask, 'Where's Summer? Why didn't you bring her? You shouldn't go off and leave her there alone. She might act staunch but it's her first — inside she'll be terrified.'

Well, so is Andrew. Terrified. 'We don't have to . . .' he'd tried. 'I mean, I'm not sure that we've really thought this through.'

'No,' she'd said, clutching her ears as if he was shouting. 'No, I'm having this baby. With or without you.'

'With me,' he'd said very fast, remembering his life before she was with him. 'You're having it with me.'

The life he remembered? Towels and t-shirts flap ragged and sodden on the rotary line while unwashed jeans and socks and teatowels decay in buckets or curl on his bedroom floor smelling of feet and loneliness. Unpaid bills, still in their envelopes, overflow the drawer where his mother had kept placemats, serviettes and serviette rings.

Summer had worked miracles. She cleaned, for instance, the silver reflector of the little heater and its output of warmth immediately doubled. She hired a machine and washed the carpet. Andrew would reach down and stroke the pile, amazed that all it had taken was resuscitation. He would slide open bedroom drawers and stare at his clean and neatly folded shirts and jeans. As he kicked off his boots at the back door he would breathe in the smell of his home — flowers and baking. Such things are not to be cast aside lightly.

His was the first driveway she'd come to. She'd walked maybe four ks along the road, hoping a car might pass, and there was his mailbox and the driveway winding out of sight between old man pines. It was not far off dark and, even though she'd never bought into those movies about inbred yokels with high-pitched laughs and sawn-off shotguns, she found herself a stick to carry.

Andrew was still down at the yards fixing an old gate across a stretch of crumbling boards. He knew by the frenzy of Alice and Chappie's barking that this was something out of the ordinary. It was the stick that upset his dogs, but Summer had the sense to realise this and let it drop. By the time Andrew was in sight tails were wagging.

He drove her back up the road to take a look at her car. The accelerator cable had snapped. Back at his place Andrew looked for a piece of wire he could fashion into something that might do the trick in the meantime. But by the time he'd found a bit that might do it was too dark, even with the torch, to get it in place. So she used his phone to ring a friend who would come out from Christchurch, and while they waited he cleared a space on the bench and made them a cup of tea. Black because the milk was solid.

She had been driving about taking photos of the countryside. Not just the mountains, as you'd suppose, but gateways with mud churned up like frosted icing, and half-grown lambs, and pine needles and rusting old hay balers.

She showed him these the day she returned with a thank you bottle of red wine which they drank together though he'd never seen himself as a wine drinker. She'd also snapped a photo of Andrew — close up, with a self-conscious grin and a smear of grease on his nose. It was a shock to see how much he looked like his father. No one had taken a photo of Andrew since his newly-widowed mother took off, eight years before, for the Gold Coast, leaving her son in the lurch. One pair of hands where, only a few months before, there had been three pairs: two for the farm work and one for the house and the paperwork and seeing the bills got paid.

Both times she'd visited, the state of Andrew's house had flickered a look over Summer's face — a look (he'd thought) that fell just short of disapproval. On the second visit he'd watched her carefully grasp a piece of net curtain between finger and thumb and use it to scrub a small circle of kitchen window clear of grease. She'd then peered out with apparent delight though there was nothing to see but a straggly old rose bush and a wilderness of silverbeet and weeds enclosed in collapsing chicken wire.

'Who had the vege garden?'

'My mother.'

'Ah-ha.'

He'd seen that more should be said. 'These days she lives in a concrete high-rise in downtown Surfer's. A couple of plants on the balcony. Looks onto the beach.' He'd seen photos, plus his aunt had described it. So when are you coming to see us? He'd explain that he couldn't get away, on account of the work, on account of the dogs. His mother knows how it is, but her sister has never stopped asking, and now Summer's told her they'll go next year to show off the baby.

As yet they don't know what sex it is. Everyone asks, but Summer is suspicious of scans. It's like dioxin, she says. Everyone swearing it's perfectly fine until the babies start being born with hands flapping out of their armpits.

'Handpits,' he'd offered. Once she would have laughed but being pregnant had taken away her sense of humour.

Andrew is hoping for a boy. If it's a girl he'll be most dismayed and it's bound to show.

Let's face it: he's dismayed anyway. Every time he looks at Summer's grossly distended belly Andrew sees himself sliding down the snake. Back past Start (just him to do all the work) off the bottom of the board (just him doing all the work but three mouths to feed).

He wishes he didn't feel like that, but he does. You can't help how you feel. You can't even know for certain what makes you feel that way, though fear about how they're going to manage is surely rational. In the four years since she moved in, Summer has much more than earned her keep, but a baby will take all her time.

So is fear the reason he finds her grotesque? Yes, grotesque in the way of the old-fashioned sideshow freaks. His beautiful Summer has mutated into a very large egg with skinny arms and legs. Lately, when walking, she paddles those arms in a cartoonish way, like Popeye.

She wants him to be there when it's born, and that is little enough to ask, considering what will be required of her. It's not that he's squeamish — he's seen it often enough: the opening stretched like a high note to a point beyond pain, the mother's exhaustion or stoic endurance, the protrusion of unborn limb or head, squashed and surreal like a robber's face through pantihose. Each time Andrew strives for indifference, without success. What is it he feels for the ewe? Something intense and in the range of emotions between pity and contempt. When it ought to be gratitude — after all, she is making him money. He and she are, you could say, interdependent.

The philosophy of farming flesh. Summer had found it interesting. How did it feel?

What kind of question is that?

'The kind you ask a sheep farmer.'

Well, the sheep farmer's not going to answer.

The photo in which he saw himself becoming his father had shown him more than the silent power of genes. In that single snapshot Summer had brought Andrew the news that he was a grown-up man of the land, his face already engraved by an excess of sun and silence.

It was late by the time she'd finally stood up to leave that night, so he'd offered the spare room. The sheets were still on from the previous winter when Jan had locked Roger out of the house.

Roger had complained that the bed was damp enough to sprout mushrooms, but that was over a year ago and there had been lots of warm weather since.

Summer had wanted to stay — she admitted this later when they reached the stage of examining every moment of their shared history. She'd wanted to stay, but she didn't want him to get the idea she was easy.

Andrew likes thinking back to the way it began. Summer dropping in to show off her photos and her brand new accelerator, Andrew doing a fast gathering of unwashed dishes and piling them into the sink. The way he could suddenly smell the damp curdle of the house, as if he'd borrowed her nose.

He'd wondered whether the noise of their laughter would carry as far as the kennels, and whether Alice and Chappie would know what it was. Canned TV laughter was the kind they were used to.

He and Summer had laughed about his mother's bad taste in furnishings and the way his father had dropped dead at the saleyards in the middle of Lot 37. The auctioneer had mistaken Andrew's father's clawing hand, and noise in his throat, for a bid. *Hewlbid sixty-five? Six-five? Six-five we have from Marshall Penney. Going going . . .*

So many things about Summer had pleased him. Her nuggety arms, her freckles, her wild hair, her wide-stepping stride and the way her eye teeth leaned forward like strainer posts. But now she is Humpty Dumpty and it's all different. Now she embarrasses him in social situations. Not just her ridiculous belly; there's her ridiculous mouth.

Like, a couple of Saturdays back, after the match when they

were at the Calley. Summer was reading her book by the big open fire, though some of the girls were there and he'd already had a word to her about that. 'They think you're a snob,' he said. She'd gazed at him for a time before she replied.

'I probably am.'

Her book didn't stop her listening in. Not to the girls (who were down the other end of the bar throwing themselves at Curnow, the new winger) but to Arnie and Lugger and Andrew, who were up near the fire. They were talking about the Hopoate business, keeping their voices down, as you do when there's shame involved. Much as he'd like to shrug the whole thing off as Aussie grossness, Arnie was saying, the undeniable fact was that sick bugger was a Kiwi.

'Oh, come on,' Summer had said, keeping her place in the book with her finger. 'Why the pretence that you're shocked? Let's face it, you lot spend half the time out there with your heads shoved up each other's bums, so what's a finger or two?'

She must've seen Andrew's face, but she was smiling around at them all.

'It's true,' she babbled. 'You're like cats . . .' She'd stuck out her tongue and licked the air.

Dogs he might not have minded. If she couldn't shut up she should at least have said dogs.

'I mean, what's the big problem? Scared you might get to like it?'

Andrew couldn't even look around to see who else had heard. He registered what he thought were a couple of disgusted snorts. Arnie and Lugger were speechless. Andrew felt pitied. Later he tried to tell her how idiotic she'd sounded.

'Get a life,' she'd groaned. 'The fuss everyone's making — papers, TV. *That's* idiotic. People are killing each other in the Middle East, in the Sudan . . . is it? Somewhere like that . . . literally thousands of homeless boys, a whole lost tribe of them, are wandering the desert. And we're obsessing about a finger being shoved up a few rugby players' bums. Like, what's wrong with this picture?'

'League,' said Andrew wearily. 'John Hopoate plays league, not rugby.'

She's gone out the back. For a moment or two when the door is open he can hear water pouring from the broken drainpipe. Now he can see her clomping across to the shed. She's wearing his old riding coat: it scrapes the ground but at least it covers the belly. She walks with her shoulders thrust back; if she didn't she might well lose balance and nose-dive into the mud. He guesses she'll take the bike and check out the river paddocks. She's playing the martyr. He could have gone after the game has finished — quite likely he would've — though the river will scarcely have risen and in another couple of hours this rain will be starting to clear. If there's one thing Andrew knows, it's the weather here.

Four years on the land and she thinks that makes her a farmer. Most days he can tell by her face that she's making comparisons, judgements. She's a demon for work, can't help herself: each new day presents an endless succession of things she needs to do. It's mend that fence, paint this room, lay those tiles. There's not a thing in Summer's world that wouldn't benefit from a scrape or a feed or a dose or a coat of paint.

She insists she's a country girl, and, strictly speaking, it's true. She grew up in the country, yet hers wasn't what you would call a rural childhood. She lived in communes. Three different groups in three different places but each of them in the country, so she went to country schools. But there were always one or two other kids from the commune that she could hang out with in the playground, pretending not to hear the dirty hippy taunts from kids like Andrew.

'It's wasn't your fault,' Summer forgave him. 'You knew no better.'

'It wasn't even me,' said Andrew. 'We didn't get you dirty hippies in Littledene.'

He hears the bike engine turn over and imagines her hand fumbling beneath the belly to turn the key. In the ute the belly touches the steering wheel.

Summer told Andrew to get two tickets for the after-match dinner on Saturday in case she was still around. They won't get their money's worth: her stomach and bladder are squeezed up so she can't eat more than a couple of mouthfuls at any one time. And she'll be constantly running off to pee.

Was that how it was for Andrew's mother? 'Once was more than enough,' she would say to people they hardly knew, in public places.

If it comes to it she'll even miss the mud — the ripe, clutching smell of it, the squelch and glug as her gumboots wrench themselves from its sticky embrace. Summer hauls the gate open, lifting it above the sagging hinges. Andrew lives with these daily impediments as if they are inevitable. Call it laziness, or call it acceptance — as Summer at first did, when the man and his land, as an entity, pleased her beyond question or reproach. Now she is not so sure.

This land has crept into her bones, though Andrew dismisses that notion. 'The land must belong to you,' he says, 'before you can claim it as marrow.'

'It's like with children,' he told her. 'Other people's don't matter.'

'Hello!' she said. 'They matter to me.'

'Not as much. Be honest.'

'I don't know that, do I? How could I know that? And neither do you. Unless there's something you want to tell me?'

142

He wasn't listening. 'Maoris,' he said. 'Ha! The way they go on — as if they've got some kind of patent on caring about the land.'

She'd thought of saying, 'That's the way I feel when you try to tell me I can't even claim to have come from the country!' But she knew that in a sense he was right — her parents and their selectively extended families had not belonged on the land; they had simply perched there like winter sparrows, sneering at people like Andrew's father and mother for being conventional, conservative.

If Summer's bones can lay no claim to the land, why do they shake over the first sun rays brushing the mountains and the smell of macrocarpa?

She will lay no claim to the farm, she's made herself that promise. Friends, she knows, will urge her to stake out a share. It's only fair, they'll tell her. And this is true: she's worked her arse off. Harder than him. But nobody made her do it.

Like now, latching the gate and crawling onto the Big Bear. Andrew worried, at first, that she would tip it, but the hills on this farm are nothing more than adolescent swellings. Behind them the Southern Alps run the gamut from broody to swaggering, each day a different shade and mood to slice your breath away.

When and why did she start preparing to leave? Was it the baby — that floating flesh koru with E.T. features, not even the size of a mouse and already issuing orders?

Had Andrew changed or had she? Which comes first, mother or embryo? Don't ask. Press down on the pedal for a little more speed. Over the ridge and into the gully with the two old cabbage trees, branches in the arranged disorder of stag horns, a seven-pointer.

He's not a hunter; she's grateful for that. Nevertheless, their business is slaughter and that, at least, is something she'll be happy to walk away from. She remembers him saying that blood makes the grass grow greener.

She'll ask for something by way of child support. He can't

begrudge her that. She won't move too far away. A child should know its father. He will think she's leaving because of the rugby — the watching of it, the playing of it — and this will make it her fault. Already she can hear his injured voice: *If she'd just given herself the chance to take an intelligent interest . . . When in Rome, right? When in bloody Rome. I mean, she wanted to live out here.*

It's not the football. It's nothing that Summer can put her finger on precisely. All she knows is that it has to do with things Andrew says from time to time. Like the comment about Maori and the land. Perhaps not the words themselves but the glimpse they give her of someone sullen and clenched.

'So what?' offered Summer's mother, Gloria, from her new lover's home in Rarotonga. 'Honey, loosen up. We all have our faults, so have we the right to judge?'

And Summer, tossing a log, one-handed, into the fiery mouth of the woodburner, had been suddenly nine years old at their bedroom door staring across at her father in bed with Meg, the mother of Jonah.

Inflexibility wasn't the problem there, but Summer noted the similarity in her feelings on that occasion and this. *Something is wrong with this picture.*

On the slope the bike slides sideways, but only a little. There's a lamb that's got through to the wrong side of the fence and there's another lamb dead. A late arrival, stillborn, the membrane only now starting to shrink and harden. This isn't a sight she needs to be seeing. Don't look, she orders the front of Andrew's riding coat as she picks the thing up by its back shins. She looks around for the mother. That one looking? Summer places herself between the ewe and her dead baby as she drops the stiffening body into a sack.

'Now don't you go doing any dangerous shit,' Jan orders Summer. 'Just get back in there and put your feet up.'

Andrew realises that this is the first time today he has thought about what Roger likes to call the 'happy event'. His head has been full of this afternoon's match. He has a good feeling about it: just can't buy into the hype about Marist's performance this year. Sure, they've got better but some of it's just been luck. Their new captain played for King Country and Waikato — or so they say, but Old Boys now have Garth Curnow. A background in league but the guy's built like Sly Stallone, except it's the real thing: no body-building crap there. With a bit of help, no doubt, from the gene pool, for the guy's part-something. Probably Maori, though no one's asked or mentioned — you're not supposed to these days. There's all these rules about what you're allowed or not allowed to say. Summer could tell you. But the fact remains that most of those races, they're built for hard work.

Jan presses two fingers against Summer's belly, gingerly as if it might be live-wired. 'So, we'll see you at the Calley, if not before?'

Summer nods and doesn't look at Andrew. They haven't spoken this morning and these days he reads all her silences as accusations.

Jan climbs into the back seat of the Holden, squeezing the kids up to make room.

'You stay in the front,' Andrew protests, but Jan takes no notice.

Roger, having stowed Andrew's bag in the back, climbs into the driver's seat. Andrew is standing awkwardly next to Summer who, despite her Humpty Dumpty belly, suddenly looks very small and frail.

'Well . . .' he begins, waiting for something to come.

'Good luck,' she says. 'Go gettem, Tiger.' She leans forward on tiptoes to smack a kiss on his cheek as she pushes him into the front seat.

Summer shakes out a sack and takes it across to the shelterbelt to fill with pinecones. All week she's been getting sporadic contractions, not painful or even unpleasant, just . . . involuntary. The calendar says the baby is due today, but first babies tend to be late and watched pots never boil, so Summer has been quick to stifle any emerging expectation.

Nevertheless this morning when she was hanging out clothes — the weather report said cool but fine (*Yes*! shouted Andrew, punching the bedroom air) — the contraction that came was stronger and distinctly ominous. She'd had a sense of something vast and ultimately indifferent to her well-being shoving her aside and taking control. And for a horrible moment Summer had wanted her mother.

But Gloria would have been worse than useless. Summer's birth had taken place at the second Nambassa gathering, in a tent that was already occupied by three family friends, a couple of strangers and a young stoned doctor called Hughie who was in love with Meg.

It was Meg (that same Meg who had groaned and buried her face in Carl's armpit while he shooed his daughter out of the bedroom) who had told Summer how Gloria and Carl had dropped a little acid that day she was born. But it was cool (Meg again). The only person to freak out was the St John's medic, who'd arrived uninvited.

As Summer slid into the world a Wellington band was doing Van Morrison's 'Tupelo Honey'. She was eight hours too late for Elvis Costello but has never considered that to be a cause for regret.

Bending is not an easy action so Summer's pinecone bag is filling slowly. Three vehicles have gone past in forty minutes — the road is busy today. They'll all be off to the village to watch the match. Reg Mullins, next farm but one, takes a rattle thing on a stick and whirls it around. Pathetic. Reg and Milly have retired to their farm cottage and put a manager in the big house. Their son's a psychiatrist in Edinburgh. How could he walk away from this soil, this skyline? 'Broke Reg's heart,' said Andrew when Summer was new to the district and needing to be put in the picture. 'You mean,' she'd corrected, 'he was disappointed. Your son the murderer might break your heart. Not your son the psychiatrist.'

How little she'd understood.

Out through the green pine needles lie the Southern Alps. Rain has left everything damply sparkling. This morning there was not a cloud in the sky and even now there are only a few of them up there hugging the mountains. A couple of magpies yodel from the branches high above her. In spring they swoop at Summer like huge bullets.

In spring she carries a stick.

'Look,' she wants to say to her child. 'Look at this world. What could be more magnificent?'

And in that moment she knows they will not leave.

The land will provide her child with whatever the father may lack. This decision seems to have come to Summer already made, and its naked expedience shocks her. Is this what happens? You begin to reason like a mother?

Summer and her child may be robbing Andrew of a possible future with someone like Jan, who will stand on the sidelines with thermos and liniment and not mind when the taps drip and the fences sag. But he's thirty four, and unattached farmers are fair game for women who don't like the land but want what it's worth. He's much better off with Summer than one of those women.

Since she hung out the washing the contractions have taken on a discernible rhythm. She didn't mention this to Andrew. It wasn't the kind of news he'd welcome on club final day. It definitely wouldn't help his game. And what if it turned out to be a false alarm?

Besides, he hadn't asked.

The arrangement was that she'd join them later, either down at the grounds or in the tragically genteel surrounding of the Starlight Lounge. If Old Boys have won there will be a lot of shouting (words and jugs), a few people falling over and a trickle of vomit on the lavender bushes. Win or lose, the men will talk about the game and the women will talk about the men. Summer goes to these things for Andrew's sake. Four years and he's still hoping she'll learn to fit in.

As soon as Roger had driven off Summer had rung the midwife in Christchurch. A fifty-five-minute drive but that's all there was. They closed the hospital in Littledene where Andrew was born. For a few years it sat empty but now a businessman from Korea was converting it into an old people's home.

'What do you mean, he's playing rugby?' said Sheena the midwife. 'You get him off that field. Tell him he won't have to speed but you'll all feel more relaxed once that journey's behind you.'

'I might be exaggerating,' said Summer. 'I'm not actually sure they're getting closer. I'll wait a bit and see how it goes.'

Andrew had managed only one of the 'mother and partner' nights. He and Sheena hadn't impressed each other.

Having fed the dogs and three pet lambs Summer throws her packed bag into the ute and drives to the village. She can hear the supporters hollering way before she reaches the grounds. She pulls in alongside Arnie's van. *McLeod & Son* it says on the side beneath a sketch of a pig with a sweet Babe face. *McLeod & Son, Butchers.*

Jan's girl, Suzie, and another girl sit on the bonnet of a vintage truck that must have come over from Salisbury. Suzie waves out to Summer, then the two girls jump to the ground and run off. No one else has noticed Summer and from this distance it's hard to see who is who beneath the woolly hats and polarfleece jackets. A couple of die-hards still wear old-fashioned swannies down past their knees.

The referee blows his whistle. The players stop and turn towards him. They take a couple of steps, then stand solid and staring like cows. Summer picks out Andrew by the way he stands. As she looks on, the hand of fate grasps her lower body and squeezes for all it's worth. On the field Andrew's teeth flash a grin, which means they're ahead. At dinner they'll punch one another's arms and crow, *Four years running, oh yeah* and *We are the champions*. Whether she's there or not.

Gutted, Andrew tries to think of the good things: (1) Summer wasn't there to cheer when Marist converted that last crucial try. Because sure as hell she would have — out of sheer bloody ignorance. (2) He'd had the sense to grab his good clothes knowing she'd likely be late and maybe even change her mind and who could blame her? In her shoes he wouldn't want to go out. In her shoes he wouldn't want to be seen. (3) Andrew ran rings around the spotty young sharemilker who played second five-eight for Marist.

Not that Arnie — or anyone else — seemed to notice. No one, that is, except Garth Curnow. 'Mate,' he'd said, throwing a rippling arm across Andrew's shoulder. 'Well played, bro.'

Andrew's immediate instinct had been to shake the arm off. He stopped himself — you never knew these days what ordinary thing would cause offence. (You're supposed to worry about what goes down with other races, but are they expected to worry about what upsets you?) Anyway, hugging and stuff — it's not just rugby; for some it's a cultural thing — they think nothing of it. And that's how it must be with Curnow. Must mean he feels at ease with Andrew, which is good because up until now they've all found the man a little stand-offish.

And, to tell the truth, up until now Andrew has kind of had it in for Curnow. Perhaps not right from the start, but from the time he had heard Jan telling Summer that the new winger was a 'hunk'.

Not that Andrew is jealous, nothing like that. What had pissed him off was knowing that it was part of something bigger. Like, wherever you looked these days, white guys seemed to be out of fashion. Suddenly there was a rule that unless you were part Maori, or Samoan, or Spanish, or African, or even Chinese, you couldn't be cool.

Yet it's true that Garth Curnow is good looking. Andrew glances across at the winger as he breaks open a can with the youngster from Salisbury. Beneath his shorn scalp Curnow has one of those long faces that suggest intelligence. The mouth is curved, the nose slightly hooked. It could be an arrogant face if it weren't for the laughter lines that soften the eyes and furrow the stubbled cheeks.

Andrew wonders about a No. 2 cut. Would his ears look big? His fingers pick at the mud on his shirt and he watches it fall to the ground. There's a graze on his left thigh the size and shape of a pocket comb.

Summer is thinking about dope and the way it elongates time, stretching each minute to the length of several days. This is happening to her now, though she's entirely straight (if that word can be applied to something the shape of a lightbulb). Neither Summer nor Sheena the midwife is committed to a drug-free delivery. This is, after all, a public hospital where an amplitude of analgesics wait in syringes or phials to comfort Summer. She only needs to give it the nod, and perhaps this will happen, though at the moment the idea of accepting anything that might slow time even further strikes Summer as madness. She wonders about the proper-ties of acid, which she has never sampled — at least not since pre-birth. If acid, too, stretches time, Gloria must have believed, in that tent at Nambassa, that she had entered a primal, psychedelic version of eternity.

Summer has been for a walk around the gardens and looked at the pruned-back rose bushes and the chunky designer polyanthus. She's walked along every passage on all four floors, peered into every

open door. Wards, storerooms, kitchen, nurses stations, TV rooms
. . . Oncology, renal, emergency, neo-natal . . . This perpetual
striding around is a thing that mad people do and Summer would
prefer not to be doing it but seems to have no choice. It's apparently
what her baby requires right now.

The baby also wants Andrew to be with them. Perhaps Summer
wants that too — it's hard to tell where the baby ends and the
mother begins. Now that labour is definitely underway she sees that
it's not just a woman thing, the way she'd thought it would be.
There's a toll bar on the hospital phones so Sheena has driven home
to ring the Littledene pub and leave a message. Who knows if they'll
remember to pass it on, and anyway how would Andrew get here?
Summer was supposed to be driving him home.

Under the shower Andrew has to shake off a wave of dizziness. Too
many cans downed too quickly; combined, perhaps, with the
stinging bite of hot water on his raw thigh. He'd stood around
drinking with some of the lads and then with Jan and Roger and old
Reg and Millie Mullins. He was waiting for the shower block to
empty, sparing himself the forced shrugs and glazed smiles of his
teammates and the Marist victors' humming and smirking.

Andrew's going-out clothes are through on the wooden seat,
clean and folded the way his rugby gear will be when he goes looking
for it next season. He chucks his filthy gear into the laundry basket
and next thing it's all back in his drawers good as new. Amazing.
Andrew's mother was never that efficient. It means a lot. Liz Conway
has Brian taking turns, but Liz always was small minded. Summer
used to complain but now she just gets on with it.

Andrew looks up from examining his scraped thigh and Garth
Curnow is standing at the edge of the steam, naked except for a dark
towel slung over his shoulder. He is looking at Andrew and speaking
but Andrew can't hear. He cuts off the shower. Garth is gesturing

no-don't-worry but it's too late, the water is off and silence now blasts away at the both of them. Andrew notices, now the steam has cleared, that Garth Curnow has a muscular groove that runs from buttock to thigh. It's the kind of indent you see in a well-toned racehorse.

'Sorry, bud,' says Garth Curnow. 'It was nothing. Sorry, get back in there.'

Andrew unhooks his towel. 'I was getting out anyway. What was it?' He doesn't begin with his hair as he normally does but dabs at his chest like a girl hiding behind her towel.

'Nothing,' says Garth Curnow. 'Well, the baby. I said it must be pretty near due.'

'Pretty near,' says Andrew. At least it seems that those words, or words very like them, are said, but he can't be sure for Garth Curnow has stepped closer and placed one hand at the base of Andrew's neck. It is remotely possible that this is a cultural gesture but Andrew suspects not.

Garth Curnow's eyes hold no smiles, just a glittering flicker that makes Andrew think of trout and hooks. Casting, he thinks. Garth Curnow is casting a spell on Andrew.

Or maybe a curse.

Garth Curnow's lips succour Andrew in a way that Summer's never have. But when they are taken away Andrew doesn't feel nourished. What he feels is more like hunger, closely followed by a flood of despair.

'Were you surprised?'

Summer is smiling up at him. She is radiant, her face cranked several notches above happiness like an Olympic gold medallist's up on the dais with the national anthem playing. Her free hand reaches for one of his. 'I'm sorry.'

'Sorry?'

'About the game.'

Andrew has to cast his mind back; it seems so long ago. 'It doesn't matter,' he says. And it's true, it doesn't matter. It's hard to believe he ever imagined it did.

He'd taken the long route up to the pub, needing the walk. Curnow had left the changing rooms before Andrew, slipping out soft footed with an ambiguous smile. 'Don't fight it,' he'd murmured before disappearing. Andrew made an inventory of all the things that ought to have warned him — the way the man stood, walked, smiled, gestured. Why hadn't he noticed?

Maybe he had.

When he reached the Caledonian they were all at the windows, waiting, looking out. A terrible moment. But then Jan had run out saying he was maybe a father already, and Arnie behind her with the keys to his little old van. And Garth Curnow in his Hi Lux single cab with the key in the ignition and the door open. 'Andy,' he'd called.

Andrew had hesitated for just a second before jumping into the butcher's van.

Summer has been set free. From the lumbering weight of her unwieldy womb, and from the misguided anxieties that came with it. No decisions, after all, need to be made. Hormones had skewed her judgement. Still, she is pleased Old Boys lost; that way she knows for sure that it is indeed fatherhood that makes her farmer glow.

'What are you thinking?' she asks him.

He takes a moment. 'Lambs,' he says. 'I was thinking of lambs.'

This makes her smile.

Yes, lambs, he thinks. As in Lamb of God, and Blood of the Lamb. As in miracles. He has a son. He is a red-blooded man. In his moment of need, this child has arrived to save him.

REASONS AND OTHER
EXCUSES

I'm not saying it's all her fault. I'd never say that. Fair enough, I was the one doing wrong, but all the same, she brought a lot of it on herself. She really did. She's soft, and the fact is she handled things badly.

At the start she'd cry, which wasn't much use, and she'd ask me what I thought she should do. Me. As if I knew. And, if I did, as if I was going to tell her. I'd say how sorry I was and how it wouldn't happen again. And at the time I most likely meant it. But a few months and I'd be at it again, telling myself that this time she wouldn't find out.

And if she did, so what? You see what I mean? All she'd do was cry or moan at me.

'You'd moan if your arse was on fire,' I told her.

'What's that supposed to mean?'

'Just what it says — you'd moan about anything.' I hadn't ever thought about what it meant; it was just something my mum used to come out with all the time.

'That's not what it says.' Typical of her, always poking and prodding at words as if there was something suspicious inside them. 'You mean instead of doing something about it? Is that what you mean? What am I supposed to do? You're the one with the problem.'

Problem. You see? Problem. That's how she saw it right from the start. And a problem, for her, was something you talked about. And talked about. And talked about.

'Why did you start?' she wanted to know. 'How does it make you feel?'

Didn't I understand that, overall, I never would win? The government was winning by way of the taxes and the people who owned the machines were no doubt winning up large. But not the fools like me out the front feeding the money in.

I thought, how would she know? She's not into winning, hardly at all. It was no fun playing anything with her. I'm one of those people who like a challenge. I don't take kindly to being beaten. You have to care. You have to have that burning coal in your gut that makes you keep on trying until you get what you're after. That's why I got where I did. Signing autographs, all of that. Hadn't of been for my leg I'd still be out there.

After a time she came to that same thought, but from a different direction. Was it because of my stuffed-up knee and what I'd missed out on?

This was her second try for something to blame. The first — surprise, surprise — was my childhood. She was so sure she was right on that one she got into a shitty when I put her straight. So then I went along with her theory. She was dead set on finding a reason, and if that made her happy why not? You might say that, in my ears, this was an idea whose time had come. And for all I knew she could be right.

With that bit sorted, she wanted to help me. Being helpful always cheered her up. We sliced the credit card into little pieces and dropped them in the bin. It didn't hurt a bit. And because it was a shared card, and because she was keen to help, we paid it back together, a little each week out of our wages.

And I began to think about my dad, though I hadn't for years. I imagined telling him about how she was helping me and how, together, we'd cut up the card. He'd go off his head. Instead of nipping things in the bud like she should of, there she was being nice and kind of letting me getting away with it.

We got away with nothing, us kids; the old man made sure of that. There was no talking about it, no finding excuses, no threats that never got carried out. He was the original action man: you stepped out of line and you got what was coming and a bit more besides. You knew where you were with my dad, and my mum was right there behind him, backing him up to the hilt.

And the thing is, it worked. We all toed the line.

I hated the old bugger, all of us did. But looking back I can see that by nature we were a pack of demons and it was just the two of them that kept us under control. We were a credit to them — that's how he needed it to be and that's how it was. We may have hated his guts but he had our respect. Other people's too, on account of us being such well-behaved kids. So that when we left home — and fools that we were, we couldn't get out of there fast enough — the olds fronted up to Welfare and got them some foster children. I think it was three in all, but the middle one ran away and never came back. Turned out maybe she did the right thing, but that's a matter I don't intend to go into. Let me just say that in the meantime, without Dad and Mum to keep them on the straight and narrow, some of my brothers and sisters were getting themselves into strife left, right and centre.

Anyway, it took us a while but me and her paid back the bank, every last cent, and I was good almost right till the end. But there's times you need a credit card. Everyone has one. So I went off to the bank and got one of my own, no problem. In fact they were more than happy. I had a credit record, you see, and they wanted me back in the fold.

This time it was just WHY? full stop. And I could tell that reminding her about fame-snatched-away-by-fate wasn't going to cut any ice.

Why did she think? I did it because I wanted to win. Those bloody machines — last time they'd beat me, but this was a rematch. And I'd started off like a rocket. I honestly thought this time I was in for the kill.

The thing about me is I don't give up. Take my job — if I took no for an answer I'd of got to the end of the week without making a single sale. A job like that, you've got to keep on, wear them down. Of course you get knock-backs but you can't afford to give up. Every door is another challenge. You have to believe in success, that's what they taught us. Now and again I'd get some couch potato who'd recognise me, and that was an easy sale for certain.

You could say I was meant for the job. Suited me down to the ground. No one looking over your shoulder so you can please yourself what hours you work. Lots of travelling around and wherever you are there's always a pub no more than a few blocks away.

I didn't say any of that to her. I just said I didn't know why, and I was really, truly sorry. Which I certainly was. Eight grand down the drain — who wouldn't be sorry? I think I even shed a few tears. She wanted me to ring up and get counselling but I scotched that idea. I imagined a bunch of people sitting round in a circle, much like they do in casino bars, except instead of machines in the middle there'd just be a space. Eye contact, confessions, all that

157

crap. I mean, you look at your neighbours on the machines and by and large they're losers. Not many with a competitive edge like me. Who'd want to take advice from a bunch of sad-sacks like that?

'Give me one last chance,' I said.

So she did.

An automatic payment out of my book every week. It was her who insisted on that, not the bank. At nineteen-point-something per cent the bank was laughing all the way to its overseas owners. I'd paid off maybe a third of it and they sent me a letter saying would I like them to raise the credit limit to fifteen grand.

Would I what!

Let's just say from there it was all downhill. I started inventing a few extra sales to keep the shit from the fan for a little bit longer. I must of known it was just a matter of time and I'd get found out but I wasn't thinking all that straight.

I lost my job but, would you believe, she still stuck by me. She'd been secretly educating herself on the power of the pokeys, and the people who made them were just like the bastards who made cigarettes. Only instead of nicotine they had psychologists who'd figured out all the best ways to hook people in.

My problem was I had a disease. She made it sound like something I'd caught off a slutty machine — some kind of STD of the brain. But at that point I was so far down I'd of gone along with anything. This time I even agreed to the counselling. Just one to one and I went there every week. We talked about changing my lifestyle and ways to deal with the urge.

I'd come out of his room all charged up with good intentions, I really would. And for a while it was full steam ahead. I got a new job — there's always someone needing a first-rate salesman — and she started to smile again and talk about our future.

But that summer it was stinking hot; you just had to stop now and then for a beer. And there would be some prick in there winning a fortune. The clatter of all those coins pouring out would seem to go on forever.

She packed her things and left while I was out on the job. Wasn't that hard to track her down, though. On the phone she'd sometimes cry and I'd get the feeling that, if I found the right thing to say, she'd still come back. But it didn't work out that way. She got the number changed. Then I started calling around to see her but next thing she's got some court order out and I'm banned from going there.

All this crap is interfering with my job so before you know it I don't have one any more. And then the landlord tosses me out because I'm a bit behind with the rent. I don't go back to the counsellor — well, obviously it wasn't doing much good.

I went to stay with my sister, the one who's a solo mum. She's a chip off the old block, hard as nails. She made me sign the dole money over to her and then handed me back $20 a week, passing it out like it was a pint of her own blood. The girl behind the desk at Work & Income yawned when I told her my story. Said sorry, but she heard stories like that nearly every day.

My sister had liked my lady. 'You fool,' she'd say. 'You bloody pathetic bastard. You better get your shit together soon. You're not actually welcome here in case you don't know.'

She'd have me babysitting and cooking the dinner. It was like being back at home with the olds, and I got to thinking more and more about my dad and how I'd never really appreciated the way he'd made sure we all stayed out of trouble.

So one Sunday I slipped out and went to see him. I didn't tell my sister where I was going; she'd of been dead against it. On the bus I was nervous. It was more than ten years and I didn't know how he'd be, or if he'd even want to see me. In my head I ran over what I needed to tell him. Should it be the whole story? That way he would understand why it had taken so long for me to come round to seeing things his way. Or would that be asking for trouble? Then again, what could he do? There'd be other people around.

Probably best to let him think I was a success, and all of it thanks to him.

They seemed surprised when I gave his name. I guess no one came to see him except my mum, and she'd long since passed away.

I waited in the big room and after a while they brought him in. I think he was pleased to see me — it was hard to tell. He used to be kind of scrawny but he'd muscled up, and apart from the grey hair he hadn't aged much at all. I stood up, wondering if we would shake hands or what, but he just sat down in the chair across from mine, watching me all the time as if I might suddenly disappear in a puff of smoke. So I sat down again. My mouth was dry. I swallowed and tried a bit of a smile.

'Hello, Dad,' I said, gearing up to make my speech.

He leaned towards me. 'I suppose, like everyone else, you want to know why?'

'No.' And I meant it. I thought about her and how useless *why* had proved to be. My voice came out as a whisper and he may not have heard.

'I spelt it out,' he said, and his eyes were still fixed on my face. 'I told him, but that bloody kid wouldn't listen. "If there's a next time," I told him, speaking as clear as I am to you now. "Next time I'll bloody kill you — and I mean that."' His voice had got louder and everyone else in the room went suddenly quiet. I looked around at the little group next to us. He had one arm around his lady and the other holding a little kid on his knee. When I looked they turned away.

My dad seemed to lose some of his nerve. He lowered his voice. 'I never did go making idle threats — you know that. If it was one of you kids you would'a known better. Isn't that so?'

'Yeah, Dad,' I said. 'It certainly is.'

160

'Did you ever know me go back on my word?'

'No, Dad. Never.'

'Well. There you are then.' His eyes finally moved off me and settled on the windows where through the little bars you could see the carpark.

That was when I knew I had done the right thing in coming. I reached out, because it seemed to be the sort of thing that was done in that room, and I put my hand over his.

'That bloody kid,' I said to my dad, 'has a helluva lot to answer for.'

SAVE AS

The man who walks into the bank is Jenna's father. He ambles in with a rifle slung over his shoulder and, because this is a two-bit town on the edge of a mountain range and men with rifles and dogs and utes are not an unfamiliar sight, nobody on the street takes one bit of notice.

Apart from the teller and Jenna's father the bank appears to be empty. In fact the assistant manager is in a side office with a customer, and a second teller is out the back on the toilet, but for Jenna's father, who is a beginner at bank robbing, out of sight is out of mind.

Jenna knows exactly how it was, every detail. It's as if she was there instead of a couple of thousand ks away in Miss Thoms' year two class at Junction Primary. She's never been into that bank, or visited that town. In fact she hasn't even set foot on the North Island.

(Though she will. She intends to, just as soon as Annie will let her leave school.)

The scene Jenna holds in her mind was compiled years before. The talk had gone on for weeks, grown-ups talking to grown-ups, but Jenna was good at going unnoticed. It was as if they could talk about nothing else, their voices criss-crossing that single event as if it was a playing field where something tiny but invaluable had been dropped and must be found.

In the newspapers there were pictures of Jenna's father holding a microphone and smiling, and of Jenna's father and Brooke Subritzky holding each other and smiling. The stories were tucked around the sides of the pictures, not like regular stories but in hay bales lined up side by side. Jenna was good at reading: she got gold stars.

Her father's name would leave the other words and jump up at her. *'Forest' Bennett* the papers would say. *'Forest'* with speech marks to show it wasn't his real name. Or else they wrote *Frederick*, no speech marks, though he was never Frederick, not to anyone.

The kids in her class would smuggle cuttings to school and give them to Jenna, respectfully and sometimes with a measure of envy. Jenna's father was famous even before he died. Two years earlier he and Brooke were runners-up on *Talent Time*. The band drove down to Christchurch to try out for the show. Back then they were called The Long Johns, though there wasn't a John among them. But the TV people didn't want the whole band, just Forest and Brooke, who did the singing.

Jenna was only four years old, yet she can remember watching her daddy on the TV.

The first time — the elimination round — they watched at Taua's place. There was Taua and Jenna and Sammy and their mother Annie. Their dad was meant to watch with them but he got held up. Jenna remembers her mother screwing cigarettes into the ashtray one after another as if it was some kind of ciggie race.

On TV Forest didn't look all that much like their father. He was dressed in a suit the colour of dry grass. Beside him was Brooke in glittering shoes and a dress that rippled and shone like a river in sunlight.

They sang 'I Got You, Babe'. Sometimes their father smiled out at them sitting there in front of Taua's TV, but mostly he smiled at Brooke and she smiled back and bounced her gold curls against his shoulder. Jenna's mother smoked her cigarette so hard they could smell the filter burning.

The woman judge liked the way they'd sung to each other. She said it had made her tingle all over. Taua snorted like a horse.

'It's part of the act, Mum,' said Jenna's mother.

'So we'll give them an Oscar,' said Taua. 'And I know just where I'd put it.'

By the time the finals were screened Jenna's father had left home and was living with Brooke in Christchurch.

'It's a career thing,' Jenna's mother would tell people. 'They can pick up regular work in the city.'

'As I recall,' snapped Taua, 'he had a regular job right here.'

This was true. Right up until the finals of *Talent Time* Forest was leading hand for Patterson Silvaculture. He had worked in the bush since he was Freddy Bennett, sixteen years old, a school and family dropout.

'Waste of a good bushman,' sniffed Taua.

But nothing was wasted, that was easy to see. The years of working outdoors had given Forest's skin the dusky purplish glow of a damson plum. And the years of climbing hills and ladders, and wielding massive pruners and hand saws, had given Forest the kind of legs and arms that got a man noticed when he went on TV.

Soon Brooke and Forest were doing so well that they asked the rest of the band to come down and join them. Lesley, who played the fiddle, hugged Annie under the clothesline.

'I'm sorry,' she squeaked. 'Will you ever forgive me? I feel such a traitor but Jeff says he's going with or without me.'

'Will you still be The Long Johns?' asked Jenna's mother.

Lesley made a face. 'The Environment. Brooke, Forest and the Environment. It's not very country and western.'

Every two or three weeks their father would drive up to see Jenna and Sam and to say a few uneasy words to their mother who straight away would turn into a statue, the kind with a thin wooden face and long eyelids and no ears at all. Then he would take Jenna and Sam for a short ride in his car, a convertible and fancier than any car they'd ever been in.

Once, when Sam had tonsillitis and couldn't come, and after Jenna had crossed her heart and promised not to tell, they drove out of town to a pub and out came Brooke with her jumpy green eyes and shining hair and wild fat-soled shoes. They bought ice-creams (the expensive ones, Moritz) and ate them down by the river. Her father and Brooke held hands and said *darling*, and *my love*, shoving the words around in their mouths like boiled lollies. Jenna didn't mind a bit, for Brooke was all the Spice Girls rolled into one.

She asked her father to come and sing in front of her class and a few weeks later he did. Not just Jenna's class but the whole school. Her dad on his own with his old cowboy guitar, and the teachers up behind him on chairs. The headmaster said Forest Bennett had put The Junction on the map.

Brooke had been waiting in the car and dropping her butts over the top of the door. They lay in a heap like firewood. She wasn't as friendly to Jenna as she had been the time before.

Not long after that, Forest and Brooke moved to Auckland because that was where you got noticed. He could no longer come to visit, but he rang once or twice.

The town — the bank — was some three hours' drive from Auckland. No car was found and if he'd travelled by bus carrying a rifle someone would surely have seen and remembered. Same if he'd hitched. Unless he'd had a pack in which the rifle could have been hidden, but no such pack was found.

Brooke Subritzky said that their Escort convertible had been in their driveway all that time and she was at home in bed with a migraine. She hadn't seen Forest since the night before when they'd argued and he'd stormed out. Upset, she had taken some sleeping pills. Brooke's brother, who was sharing the flat, owned the rifle, which he had stored on top of his wardrobe. On that particular morning her brother, who wanted breakfast, had twice woken Brooke but both times she'd drifted back to sleep.

Jenna learnt all this from a story headed *Beautiful Brooke grieves for Forest*. She kept that magazine under her mattress until her mother found and burnt it.

Forest walked into the bank and said, 'Excuse me, but I need your money. Please put your hands in the air.'

'He couldn't have been more polite,' the teller was quoted as saying. 'But there was also the gun.' She put her hands up. Not high in the air but raised from the elbows, and she told Forest they didn't have much cash — most of the money was locked away in the safe, which she couldn't open. Forest asked how much was 'not much', and she said very little: Tuesday mornings were always quiet and most people used the machine outside. But she would have a look, she told him; she was happy to have a look. And that was when she pressed the alarm bell. He didn't know she'd pressed it. It was the kind of alarm that only rang in the police station.

There was just one officer at the station — the other had nipped down to the bakery to pick up their morning tea — and he was a young officer, torn between fear and excitement. He took a gun and detoured past the bakery just as the senior officer emerged with cream doughnuts.

The younger man was first into the bank. He saw Forest with

the rifle, and the teller pushing a small bundle of notes across the counter towards him. 'Drop the gun,' he ordered.

He waited. It felt to him like a long time, though of course it wasn't. Eventually Forest turned around. He was still holding the rifle and the barrel was aimed at the officer, whose name was Barry McCrostie. The officer fired.

Forest had never been a hunting man. No one could recall even seeing him with a gun. The rifle he took to the bank wasn't loaded.

There was a lot of arguing over whether or not officer Barry McCrostie was to blame. But what difference did it make? Jenna felt sure that, under the circumstances, her father wouldn't have minded dying. Dying probably didn't feel so much different from singing on TV. What counted was how well you did it.

Forest and Brooke were not like most other people; they were deeply in love. Which is to say that love had taken them over. They were in its possession. Not many people are capable of falling deeply in love, but Jenna feels a deep certainty that some day it will happen to her. She can hardly wait. She longs for silver boots up to her thighs, dark alcoves and droplets of blood. She dreams of knives slicing through stones and when she wakes up she finds that her body is trembling of its own accord.

It's a Saturday in May, and if you get out of the wind there is still heat in the afternoon sun. Jenna can feel it on her back, angling in through the glass doors, as she sits at Annie's computer. She's meant to be writing a critique of *The God Boy*. But instead she's messing around with the fonts, trying to choose between 𝕭𝖑𝖆𝖈𝖐𝖆𝖉𝖉𝖊𝖗 𝕴𝕿𝕮 and **Arial Black**.

A car — a boring, dusty Japanese type — turns in at the driveway and a boring, dumpy little woman gets out and stands shivering in the wind. Then she sees Jenna and waves and heads for the ranchsliders.

167

'Jenna? Is it Jenna? Oh yes, you're his spitting image. Do you remember me?' Uninvited, she slides the door open. 'Lesley?'

'Yeah.' Jenna stands up, pleased to be interrupted. 'Course I remember you.' There was Forest, Brooke, Lesley, Jeff and Pete. 'You kind of look different.'

'I've got fat. You can say it: it doesn't bother me.'

Liar thinks Jenna. She says, 'Mum's at work. Till about lunch time. Why don't you wait? Unless you're in a terrible hurry or something?' Jenna doesn't want to get back to *The God Boy* assignment. She hates critiquing — even the word is wanky. 'I could make you a coffee.'

'A glass of water would be fine.'

Lesley follows her through to the kitchen. 'I can't get over . . . how old are you now?'

'Fourteen.'

'And . . . your brother?'

She can't remember Sam's name. Jenna is pleased to learn that her brother is unmemorable.

'Sam. He's out, thank God. And Jeff?' she adds, to show that *she* remembers.

'We split up,' Lesley is at the window. 'The year after we left here. He's got a Japanese wife now and a couple of kids. Yoko, I call her.'

She grins at Jenna, who feels obliged to smile but keeps it brief. Yoko means nothing to Jenna but she suspects racism. Maybe this shows, for Lesley now babbles.

'Her real name's Daphne. She's a systems analyst, whatever that is. And actually, to be perfectly honest, I quite like her.' A little self-conscious laugh. 'So how's Annie?'

'She's good.' Jenna hands Lesley her glass of water. She's added lemon and ice so it looks like a real drink. Two glasses. They carry them back to the sun in the front room. There is a question in

Jenna's head screaming for attention. She waits until Lesley is seated in the wicker chair, or at least perched on the front of it so her lace-ups can still touch the ground. Jenna tries for off-hand.

'What ever happened to Brooke? You got any idea?'

Jenna had kept an eye and an ear out, anxiously. She was certain, in those first months, that Brooke would determine to die — if not from grief then by her own hand since that is what deeply-in-love demands. But after a couple of years Jenna found herself flicking through magazines in the hope that Brooke would be featured, as beautiful as ever. *Putting tragedy behind her and picking up the shards of a shattered career.*

This hope remains. Jenna's dream is of locating Brooke by the time Annie lets her quit school. This is likely to take place in an overseas city like LA or Vegas. Despite the courage she's shown in resuming her career, Brooke's heart can never be truly mended, so Jenna's arrival will cause her pain along with the joy.

Lesley is saying with venom, 'I know what *should've* happened to her. She should've been done for murder. And, yeah, funnily enough, I do know what happened to her. We ran into each other just last year in Queenstown. I thought right away *I'll have to tell Annie.*' Lesley hesitates; the look on Jenna's face is making her nervous.

'So? Tell her what?'

Lesley shrugs uncertainly. 'We were in a restaurant. She was there with her husband.'

'Husband?'

'She introduced him. They live in Tauranga. I think it was Tauranga. I wouldn't've recognised her but she came over.'

'Brooke Subritzky?'

'Grey hair in a little bob. A kind of grey top and clingy trousers and, honestly, she's as fat as me. You wouldn't look twice at her.'

Lesley's eyelashes are stubby and pale. Her belly rests on her thighs and her hair is shapeless and greying. Jenna thinks it's no wonder Jeff went off with someone neat and clearly defined.

Lesley leans towards Jenna. 'I certainly didn't act pleased to see her. I wouldn't do that to you and your mother.'

'They were in love,' Jenna says softly but clearly. 'My dad and Brooke were in love.'

'They were in debt, more like.' Lesley is watching Jenna closely. 'Brooke had expensive tastes.'

For a moment Jenna is in a big echoing room — perhaps a gymnasium — on her own, and then she is back with Lesley. 'You don't know,' she says in a flat voice, not looking at Lesley.

In silence Jenna finishes her glass of water and fishes the slice of lemon from the bottom of the glass. Outside, two of her classmates ride past on horses. She doesn't look out in case they are looking in. Finally she says in a small voice, 'They *were* in love.'

'Forest was,' says Leslie. 'He was in love, and he was a fool.'

Jenna watches the ever-changing pattern of the screensaver, the colours that blend and merge. 'I think you should go now,' she says.

Lesley looks startled. She gets to her feet and thrusts her empty glass at Jenna. With dignity she steps out into the chill wind.

From her computer stool Jenna watches the car back out of the driveway. The feel of the mouse beneath her palm is oddly comforting. She can see her face — so much resembling her father's — reflected in the screen. Jenna guides the cursor up to the menu and considers her options. Save. Change to. Delete. Save as.

COWBOYS

I spend a lot of time thinking why. As if there has to have been one absolute reason, and if only I could single that out, everything would come clear and I'd know, now, what to do.

Remembering back then. One single reason? I test the contenders in my head.

Q. Why?

A. (a) *I always liked cowboys.*

And there he was — the real thing. On the forms he puts pensioner, but even these days you look at him, you see a cowboy. Which has to do with being loose but hard. That's what I saw at the start. A body like stones, hair in tight curls — what was left of it — a frizzled ridge on which his stetson balanced. Eyes tight too, in a squint from many far horizons. Even, years later, when his sister showed me photos, my eyes embellished and I saw the wide-brimmed hat and the legs bowed in expectation of a saddle.

(b) I was looking for a father figure.

The common theory. Everyone, back then, adding and subtracting. So much fuss about his age. And mine. But to me he had no age. He was just a human being at some point between cradle and grave. Besides, I had a real sense that I had always been older than him.

(c) I was young (certainly) and stupid . . .

Some days I settle for that. Those days when I know it to be true, and see only that there is no hope for us and remember how it was being fourteen and having this life, just one life, and no one you can believe in to tell you what to do with it. And there I was, a kid who loved horses — all horses, but not so much the soft-eyed, obedient kind. I liked impatient mouths, the quick dark spread of sweat, the edgy high-stepping hooves, a flash of white in the eyes. I despised easy.

And there he was, in this old cottage down the road, with a stallion, two mares, four dogs and a couple of toddlers. A cowboy on the DPB. Someone more than three-dimensional, sliding in and out of myth.

I'm the one who's changed. Four kids. Who wouldn't change? His first two — those toddlers — older, now, than I was then. Fourteen, and still intact. I'm not talking maidenhead (that matter of so much legal and prurient concern) but mind. At fourteen I was singular and certain. At thirty I am divided. Two minds, two selves, two lives.

This one: We're in the Valiant, all six of us. The kids in the back, not yet squabbling. Already the dust rises up around us, though it's early and the heat has yet to come. We're driving south, away from home, away from the baked and shrinking soil, the endless whittering babble of the chooks and ducks and guinea fowls, the axe poised on the chopping block, the hole in the bathroom wall. He is driving, his hat pushed back, and talking with the kids in the way he does, weighing up their words as if each thought they have is the wisest, most profound thought to have hit the universe. I watch the road from habit, dodging in my mind the biggest stones. Then I remember that shops mean people, so I fish through the mess in the dashboard till I find a comb to pull through my hair. And they clamour in the back to comb their own their brother's their sister's hair, so I pass it over and as I do he begins to recite. One of those loping Australian poems he loves, Banjo Whatsits — one of those. And not for one moment do I think about New Zealand — the hills, the cabbage trees, the pennyroyal smell of a summer river. I watch the red Aussie dust settle and I am entirely happy.

Then there's this one: Morning again. We sit out the front drinking tea. We watch the baby cram the last of her scrambled eggs into her grinning mouth. She likes an audience. Just like her father, I'm thinking when the dusty white ute comes into view. Ray and Merrill. I sigh. He gives me a grin, but all the same I see his body perking up. Like his dogs, who already are straining on their leashes.

Merrill is talking as she and Ray hop out of the ute and their two kids scramble down from the back. Ray reaches behind the cab and lifts a full crate. He carries it across on his shoulder. Merrill is ahead of him, filling us in. Last night they went to a party at Gravesend, stayed the night. Thought they'd detour this morning, see how we were. *Great*, he's saying. *We're real good. And you're looking well yourself, Merrill.*

I'm looking at those bottles, still dewy with condensation, and thinking that they didn't bring those all the way from Gravesend, they must be open at Woodridge. Which means half the morning gone already and here Ray is, about to seize the rest of our day. Their kids have taken off already, joined up with our three out the back. Merrill lifts the baby from her highchair, wipes her face with the bib and slaps kisses all over her face. Merrill wants another baby but Ray thinks two's enough. Ray takes out his fancy pocketknife and opens bottles. I go inside to make another pot of tea.

The littlest two are asleep, the rest are hungry. I butter bread in the kitchen, which is dark and almost cool. I can hear his voice in full swing, charging like a steam train on and on, that compulsive rhythm, and their laughter, over and over. I butter bread and look around me with eyes that are not mine, and I see poverty and ugliness. I see ash seeping from the woodstove grate and the broken wallboards. I see the microwave that I'd wanted so badly because everyone else had one, its shelf propped up with bricks, and I see how ridiculous it looks, not belonging. *God help me, what am I doing here?*

And this chilly visitor that stares from my eyes tells me in her scornful voice how the rest of this day will go. The beer will run out but money will be found, and pooled, for more. And for the petrol to get them to the liquor store and — eventually — back. And tomorrow's food will be eaten tonight by four extra mouths; he will insist, the soul of hospitality. If Merrill is sober enough they will leave, eventually, driving into the night with their children wrapped in borrowed blankets. Please let her be sober enough. And he and I will turn back into the front room where the TV's going and empty bottles lie on the floor beside the baby's discarded dinner, and then he will see for sure this stranger looking out from my eyes and this will fill him with rage. And if I am cunning and fast I'll get out of that room and find somewhere to hide. But we've been here seven years now and I'm running out of places.

Merrill comes in to help me. We slice cold mutton and tomatoes and she keeps her voice down, telling me about her and Ray and the night before. It's the piss, she says: if it wasn't for that he'd never lay a finger on her. Last year, she says, he fractured two of her ribs. Drunk as. They're all the same, she says in her harsh

Aussie voice, all his mates — can't wait to get drunk and when they do they go right off. She gives me a prompting look but the stranger inside me ignores it. I stack the sandwiches on a plate.

Mine like the crusts cut off, she says.

I hide, this night, behind the dog kennels. Half-hearted because I figure he's ready to collapse. I'm grateful for the warm night and the skinny new moon. A perfect land, this, for hiding out from drunks. I wonder how many of us there are *at this moment* crouching in the darkness. The stranger has moved out of my head. I'm calm and slightly bored and I have an urge to laugh. I think about Merrill, who has a ninety-minute drive on mesmerisingly straight roads, and feel bad about not even having said to her *I know*.

I transport myself to the ute, a seat crammed with sleeping bodies. Merrill upright, staring out at the gravel road rushing towards her in the tumbling headlight. I whisper to her that I am currently, pathetically, crouching behind the empty dog kennel. And I laugh, because you have to.

I don't know what I expect from Merrill, but it's not . . . definitely not . . . this look of satisfaction.

PARENTAL LEAVE

The corridor is pale grey, satin finish, with glossy cerise fittings. Someone has chosen those colours from the spectrum of colours and shades, and she (he?) was bent on avoiding the sins of the past. That's what these corridors say to Ursula. Not too shiny, they say. Not too bland. Not too obviously institutional. She feels a glow of gratitude for this attempt to make her feel a little less awful.

Three doors along there is a room where she could stare at magazines, make instant coffee or chat with a woman whose peach-coloured dressing-gown hangs like stage curtains either side of a heavily bandaged stump.

The nurses keep pointing Ursula in the direction of that room — a hot drink, make yourself at home, sing out if there's anything . . . She thanks them, shaking her head. In the corridor she can keep an eye on his door. And she can pace — which is how she knows about the woman with the stump sticking out of her dressing gown like a huge cigar-shaped penis. If Ursula was to sit in there she might giggle; her self-control feels tenuous.

At the far end of the tasteful corridor a new baby sends out a purple scream of rage or pain. *Too soon*, thinks Ursula in dismay. *It's come too soon.* The words are there in her mind as if she's invited them, but why would she? She has no particular faith in reincarnation — no more than in any of the other theories. Even Darwin; how could anyone know for certain?

Yet, hearing that scream, some part of her takes it for granted that an unknown infant had arrived like a taxi to collect her father. A taxi that came too early. Unless . . . but no, the nurses are with him; they would surely let her know.

Perhaps the baby has come expecting to wait. A newborn child is really nothing more than functioning flesh plus reflexes. The brain takes months — years, in fact — to develop. At first the eyes can't even focus. Look into them and there's nothing. No individual human essence. Okay — no soul.

For months after her mother died Ursula had found herself looking with too much interest at any butterfly that landed within her reach. Even the occasional snail. Not to mention a grey and white kitten who pretended homelessness. Yet her mother's life had been full and happy. She'd said so herself. 'I've been very, very lucky,' she'd said, as if bits of her memory had been deleted.

Ursula's mother had no need to come back, but her father has every reason. Her father needs a second chance.

She hears the baby's screaming, rendered thinner and possibly sharper by walls and distance, and then she hears the coughing begin so close and jagged it seems like her own lungs. (If only it could be. Even just once to give his a rest.)

The coughing means he is back in the room. Maybe not yet in bed but standing, a nurse beneath each arm, waiting for the spasm to pass. Waiting in that patient way nurses have, at least in public, while outside Ursula waits in the way she would wait for an earth-quake to cease — fearfully and without confidence.

He hates her to see him coughing. He hasn't said so, but then he wouldn't; he's long out of the habit of saying what he feels or wants or doesn't want. Though Ursula can remember — or thinks she can — an outgoing man with a strange honking laugh who recited rhymes by Ogden Nash and A.A. Milne. King John was his favourite. The foolish, unloved sovereign who got — purely by accident — more than he deserved. Whereas her father got much less.

Is that how he sees it? Does he look upon all those years as penance? Or is he in fact happy enough, unregretful?

Any day now, the red-haired nurse said last night. But Ursula knew that already, had seen for herself. Back in his room she'd taken his long knobbled fingers into her hand and locked them there, as if that way she could stop him leaving.

Forever — that was the word that clogged up her throat. She couldn't cope with 'gone forever'.

Ursula considers heaven. Lush green hills reflected in an indigo sea and her mother on the shore gathering driftwood, stacking it for a fire. She is wearing the dark blue dress with the scooped neckline and long flared skirt. The fabric is scattered with tiny white, yellow-centred daisies that mutate on either side of the seams. Her mother is plump again, solid and smooth, and her dark hair is pinned up in vague handfuls.

Suddenly he is also there on the beach. An old man with his trousers rolled to just below the kneecaps, his feet in the water flashing like upturned flounders, his hair as fine and feathery as a baby's. He is wearing a plaid shirt, torn at the sleeve and frayed at the collar. Ursula remembers the shirt from her last visit.

'He dragged it back out of the rubbish bag,' Rosemary had hissed, steering Ursula to his wardrobe to look at the shirts she had bought on her ungrateful husband's behalf. Respectable and unworn, some of them still with cardboard under the collars. 'He prefers to shame us both in public. I tell you, if I didn't keep at him, the man would be an absolute scruff. Seems he objects to looking presentable. Mind you,' and here Rosemary's voice slid into an off-hand tone, the vocal equivalent of one raised eyebrow . . . 'Mind you,' eyeing Ursula up and down, 'I have to say that tendency does seems to run in the family.' Then she smiled. As she always smiled in the wake of her own spite.

At first, when she was young and desperate to please, Ursula had smiled back.

This morning while they gave her father his shower she'd taken a taxi to the house. He seemed to want her to do this. 'Have you seen Rosemary yet?' he'd asked last night each time he forced his eyes open to check that Ursula was indeed there at his bedside.

When she'd told him where she was going he began listing things. Pyjamas to be washed, his eye-shade brought in, the blue woolly hat for the cooler nights. How often did Rosemary come to see him? But to ask could seem like interference in a relationship he'd never required her to approve or understand.

Why did he now want his daughter to visit his wife? She could surely ask him this. But years of things unsaid have piled up and Ursula is defeated by the sheer weight of rejected sentences.

It was Carol who answered the door. She was smaller than Ursula remembered, and the hump on her shoulders looked heavier, pressing her down.

'Ursula. Actually we have met a couple of times but you won't —'

'Carol. How are you?'

'Oh, you do remember. How kind. I'm just . . . not a good time for Rosemary to be on her own. It's very sad.'

'Yes.'

'She doesn't like being alone. You've seen him — your dad? Of course you have, what am I saying? She can't bear to . . . it's just too upsetting. Just too . . . I suppose I should tell her you're here.' Carol's matted lemon cardy gave an archway view to her floral dress. Was Carol *presentable*? Or didn't it matter since she was only Carol who'd once lived next door?

What was it about Rosemary that made this inoffensive little woman choose to be her friend?

'Well, sit down, at least,' Rosemary had ordered Ursula. 'It's much too early to offer you a cup of tea. I suppose you've been to see your father. He's not the man I married, you know, that man up there. He's a totally different man, and frankly I don't feel like dragging myself all that way to visit a stranger.'

Carol was embarrassed by this announcement. She blinked a few times, then found an eyebrow to scratch so her face was no longer in view.

'Scratching again,' snapped Rosemary.

Carol's fingers froze, then wafted self-consciously down to her lap.

Rosemary turned back to Ursula. 'She wants to go and see him. She's always had a soft spot for your father. Been a widow so long she can't remember what men are like.'

To her shame Ursula had felt that trickle of camaraderie that comes from debunking men behind their backs. Rosemary and Ursula on the same side? That couldn't be. But still Ursula did not defend her father. She was silent, as he would have been and perhaps for the same reason. In the company of Rosemary, Ursula placed her words carefully, fearful of mines and sniper fire.

Rosemary is not and never will be in Ursula's summoned-up heaven. A heaven with Rosemary in it would be a contradiction in terms. Nor, logically, should her father be there. Not yet. Though that is how Ursula has longed and longed for it to be: her parents reunited, forsaking all others. Ursula loves the way those three words fit together. This time for eternity, where they will wait, with infinite patience, for their daughter to join them.

In heaven Ursula's father will wear whatever he wants to wear and do whatever he wants to do and be whoever he really is.

If that's how he'd like it to be.

Ursula and her father really know very little about each other. This could be due to lack of opportunity. It could also be lack of courage.

The coughing. That terrible splintering, rasping cough. *Enough*, she whispers to any god whose existence isn't dependent on belief. *Please. Enough. He doesn't deserve this.* He deserves fast and painless — the going to bed and simply not waking that everyone hopes for.

In which case Rosemary would have found him next day — the old man who slept in the spare room and was no longer the man she had married. She would have felt, surely, relief. Possibly joy. Free at last, and the money would now go much further.

Has he thought about this? That his wife may be waiting with some impatience for him to die? If so, is it a recent thought or one that has been with him for years? A painful suspicion or a quiet certainty that makes staying alive an act of dogged revenge?

A fast death would have left no time for things unsaid. All the same, Ursula hopes she would have wished that for him. Anything but this old-man cough, brittle as rust.

Your family? the nurses would have asked. Is there anyone you would like us to ring?

He wouldn't have known her phone number. Not even her address. Rosemary would have had to provide it from her little book with the gold-embossed cover. The one she'd had for years. The doctor, the dentist, the lawyer, the garage, and empty pages. So many empty pages. That was a long time ago, but no reason to think anything's changed. So few people meet with Rosemary's approval.

Ursula has no reason to hope that finally she and her father will have a meaningful conversation. He was never much of a talker; Rosemary did it on his behalf. Was that it — her mother not having had enough to say? Not definite enough. Short on opinions. Weak men seek out strong women, isn't that so?

Is it weakness to endure, to live with your mistakes?

Does he regard this marriage as a mistake?

Does Ursula only see what she chooses to see?

The coughing has stopped. She's still waiting for it to start up again when the younger nurse opens the door.

'He's all set.' Her face is broad and serene. It suddenly smiles. 'That's one sweet old dude.'

'Yes.' Ursula smiles back. 'Yes, he is.'

She takes a moment to wipe her eyes on the sleeve of her jersey in case he finds her tears upsetting. She hadn't cried last night on seeing him there all shrunken and pale and pleated like some discarded piece of cloth. Right up until that moment of seeing him she'd been telling herself it was very likely a false alarm.

How long since anyone cried for him? Perhaps he needs to see her tears.

The second nurse is setting the blinds against the glare of sunlight. He will not feel the sun again.

The tears have returned but he isn't looking; he seems unaware that she's there. His eyes are open but their backs are turned; that's how it feels. She thinks it might be the drugs taking his mind off the pain by staging some kind of performance inside his head. She returns to the chair and reaches for his hand.

His eyes turn slowly back. 'They let you away, then? The job?'

Three times now. 'Yes, Dad. No problem.'

'I'm not much company.'

'You think I'm here to be entertained?'

'Should've brought a book.'

'I have. For when you're asleep.'

His fingers tighten briefly on hers. She tries to remember the things that should have been said long ago. An accumulation of unspoken words from right back when she'd stood in the dark passage watching her mother bashing her head against the mantelpiece. Back to the whywhywhy and the howcouldhe?

Back to when the holiday visits began. Three summers running, Ursula had stayed with her father and Rosemary, each time for just four days. 'Four days and any normal child is bored to tears with adult company,' Rosemary used to say. She also used to say:

'A busy child is a happy child.'

'Who would let a child wear *that*?'

'Plain little girls must learn to be useful little girls.'

And 'Who takes after her mother? Peas in a pod!'

Her father taught her chess. 'Take that pawn and you'll lose your rook. See. You have to be always thinking ahead or you'll get slaughtered.'

'Rosemary suffers from nerves,' her father would say. 'Sometimes that makes her say things she doesn't mean.'

'That's silly,' her father would say. 'How could she hate you? There's nothing about you to hate.'

Almost like saying she'd made it up.

Her mother said she didn't have to go back. 'I should never have let you go there,' she said. 'That woman . . .'

'He's scared of her,' said Ursula.

'Don't start feeling sorry for him,' said her mother. 'He got what he wanted. He made his bed.'

Ursula didn't go back to her father's house until she was earning

183

enough to pay for a motel. Neither her father nor Rosemary said it was silly for her to pay for a room when they had two to spare. Yet later, when they'd turned one spare bedroom into an office and her father had moved into the other, Rosemary had said what a pity it was that Ursula had to pay for a motel. If only they still had the spare bedroom, said Rosemary. It was the snoring, she said. Fat men did tend to snore. Had Ursula been shocked to see how he'd piled on weight? He'd needed a whole new set of clothes and the cost was outrageous. Thirty dollars just for a pair of pyjamas, would you believe.

Her father had already turned away, plodding ahead of them into the living room that was only used when visitors called, so you might as well say not used at all. Ursula sat down on the edge of a white lounge suite she would have remembered. Her fingertips told her leather.

'New,' she said, injecting her voice with admiration.

Her stepmother giggled and leaned close. 'He doesn't know yet how much it cost him. He'll have a seizure.'

Ursula moved up a rung into management. It meant more travelling and further afield. At least three times a year she was in the area. By then her father had retired so she could call in on a weekday, but she always rang a few days before to arrange a date and time. Mid-afternoon suited Rosemary best; she would turn on Devonshire teas, with whipped cream and boysenberry jam. She would lean forward in her chair watching Ursula eat. 'Have another,' she'd say. 'Go on, spoil yourself. They're your father's favourite.'

'They are too,' he'd mumble. 'When it comes to scones, Rosemary's a bit of a dab hand.'

His eyes have settled on her with what feels like puzzlement. The impersonal interest of a stranger.

'Would you like some water?' she offers. 'Some juice? Maybe an orange? I could peel . . .'

Shaking his head. His eyelids are so defined, so carefully etched they could be carved in clay. His eyes brim with liquid, but old eyes water, isn't that so?

His hand tightens on hers, tugging. 'I'm sorry,' he whispers. 'I'm sorry, lass. You know what I'm saying?'

'Yes, I know. It's okay,' she says. 'It's okay, Dad. Really it is.'

Finally Ursula knows what she wanted so badly to know. After all these years. Bits of her life swivel and slide and slot into place. Her heart glows, her tears slide.

'What's the time?' he whispers.

'Almost lunchtime.'

'This afternoon, did you say . . . Rosemary coming?'

'She said she'd most likely pop in.' (After she'd been to the hair-dresser, and if she felt up to it.)

Ursula watches her father's face compress, his eyes withdraw.

'Tell her I'd sooner she didn't. You'll do that for me?' His eyes are back again, reading her face, the reluctance, 'Urse? Say I'm not up to it if you like. Or just — I don't want to see her. Please?' *For a dying man.* He might as well have said it.

She feels her heart rise like a fist. Victory.

She imagines the phone ringing in the cramped little room where visitors don't get taken. She sees Carol answer and hand the phone to Rosemary, whose off-white merino wool cardigan (and now Ursula clearly remembers from this morning, though at the time she'd barely noticed) is wrongly buttoned. The buttonhole side hangs down like a dropped jaw and all the buttons skew-whiff. Carol glances and smiles in a knowing way. Just as she did this morning.

Carol not at all fond, but hoping to inherit? Rosemary reaping what she has sown?

On the shores of heaven Ursula's mother closes her eyes and rubs a stump of smooth white driftwood against her cheek. Then her eyes fly open and, instead of placing the stick on the pile, she laughs and swings it around her head. Once, twice she spins it, then hurls it out to sea.

The infant is crying again. Or perhaps it is another one, blood-smeared and brand new.

Ursula looks into her father's sunken eyes. 'I can't,' she says firmly. 'I'm sorry, Dad, but I can't. You really do need to tell her yourself.'

MOON LANDINGS

'Oh yes,' he murmurs. 'Oh yes, oh God.' Just like they do on those videos. And his freckles meld and blur like the Milky Way, and even though you've seen them like this, an eyelash away, at least as many times as you've gazed at the stars, they remain unfamiliar. Given a felt-tipped pen and a blank sheet of paper you would be able to replicate neither freckles nor stars.

Except, that is, for that one high on the cheekbone, which is darker and raised. That one you keep an eye on in case it changes. Monitoring the behaviour of that particular dark spot is your responsibility. These days he does not linger in front of the mirror; his glance goes mournfully to his waistline. Suck in, relax, shrug.

'Oh yes, oh shit, oh God.' And his glazed and bulging eyes tell you he's left the shuttle and is out there, weightless in a silver suit. And your brain, right now, should be inactive, a cranial cavity stuffed with dark olives and chocolate and small sharpened teeth, but it isn't.

(Feel free to replace those images with others you may prefer. But don't get too specific; with the passage of time and on closer inspection those jagged, salty images of sin dissolve into puddles of silly slime. Conjecture is more libidinous than cognisance. Portions of life should remain cordoned off and enticingly signposted: *Do not enter. Danger.*)

'Yes, now, oh yes, oh yes.' Shouting.

Your neighbours may have snatched up phones and already be dialling. Perhaps with reason, for you are anxiously watching his gulping face. An apprehension there you've never felt for the freckle/mole. Because men of a certain age die this way. At this exact moment his heart may choose to attack. He is out there taking giant strides on a primordial surface. The link to life is, at best, tenuous.

Come in, Major Tom.

This is not the kind of danger you had in mind.

For better or worse you need to be in his head right now. What's it like out there? How does he feel? What does he see?

It drives you crazy that he could die inside you while so far away. Not even a satellite link.

You are aware of a thudding heart that may or may not be yours, and of the absence of gravity.

LIES

Tom toured the country, from Bluff to Kaitaia, with Bailey's Circus. He fastened guy-ropes and scrubbed down elephants and sold tickets for the octopus ride. The elephant trainer was a woman, though she could've passed for a man. She taught Tom how to make an elephant kneel. Simple, really: you used hand signals.

Tom demonstrates with those pale, narrow hands that Andrea finds so appealing.

Carl asks, 'So when was this, Tom?'

Carl's interest appears to be genuine, but Andrea thinks she hears an edge of disbelief. She looks down to her glass where a fragment of something pinkish-white — a rose petal? — floats on the surface. Tom is saying it was the year he quit school.

And maybe it was. Sometimes these stories turn out to be true, even those that seem the most far-fetched. Where Tom is concerned Andrea lives in a state of suspended judgement.

Do the others believe him? She can never tell. People are really so polite. Each time Andrea waits, as she's waiting now, for someone to say, 'Oh, come on, Tom. That's bullshit. You're making it up.'

But of course that won't happen, and if it did, Tom would never admit to even a modest amount of exaggeration. Deftly he would camouflage and distract. Only later, when alone, would Andrea see the inconsistencies, the lack of logical connections, in those swift verbal manoeuvres.

Deep inside Tom there must be something raw and restless that compels these inventions, but Andrea has all but given up on excavation. She tries, now, to think of him as a magician, skilled in sleight of tongue. Bewildering, sometimes embarrassing, but essentially harmless.

Andrea dips a finger into the glass and removes the floating thing. *The mote from one's own eye*, she thinks.

Mary can remember when they had freak shows at the Masterton A & P. The tattooed woman, the fat man, the three-legged woman. Mary was very young and not allowed in those tents but she and her brother would stand outside gawping and once were rewarded by a glimpse of an arm fat as a rolled-up eiderdown.

'Duvet,' she amends, aware that she and Carl are the senior couple here. 'A rolled-up queensize duvet.'

Mary is talking fast in order to move the conversation on and away from Tom and Carl. She hopes she was the only one who noticed, and she hopes Carl will leave it at that. It's not like Carl to put someone on the spot, but Mary knows how he feels about Tom. He told her on the drive over.

'Makes you feel like taking him aside and letting him know he's making a dick of himself.'

'I'm sure someone's done that.'

'Not necessarily. It's much easier not to.'

'I doubt that he'd thank you for it.'

'Notice it's never something you can easily disprove?'

'Could all be true, then. We haven't known them all that long. Andrea gets that glazed look.'

'We all do,' said Carl, and Mary laughed.

She can still feel that laughter and the rush that came with it. A great gusting sense of her own good fortune in having this man who could still make her laugh, in having a car with an open sunroof and cushioned suspension, in the clear blue sky and the prospect of a long Sunday lunch in Lee and Bruce's impeccable garden.

'I guess it's harmless,' she'd said, magnanimous in her bounty. 'Just inventions. Just one step along from exaggeration, which all of us do from time to time.'

'Not me,' said Carl virtuously, and for a short while they travelled in grinning silence.

'Actually,' said Carl, back in his tracks, 'I find it insulting. Tom. Okay, he's kind of a friend and he's pleasant enough but . . . Does he think we're stupid enough to swallow his bullshit?'

Mary's talk of sideshows reminds Andrea . . .

'There was this woman . . .' She sits up straight and looks around to see that she has their attention. 'This is the saddest story. There was this monkey woman — like she was covered in hair. This is way back and I'm not sure where. America maybe, or Europe.'

'Or maybe Russia,' offers Bruce with a grin.

'Don't worry about it,' Carl tells Andrea.

'I think I saw this on-line.' Lee leans forward, chin propped between deep blue fingernails.

'It's not a joke,' protests Andrea. 'It's a true story. I read it somewhere, years ago. There were photos: she was literally covered in hair. And her family were peasant farmers, something like that, and they gave her away to this freak show. Which I suppose was a kindness, because at least in a freak show she wouldn't have felt, you know, like a . . .'

'Freak?' says Tom.

Andrea smiles nicely. 'Thank you, sweetheart. That would seem to be the word.'

Tom smiles back.

Andrea forges on. 'And for years she travelled with the show and went on display. And of course she must have longed to be just like everyone else.'

'There were razors,' says Lee. 'Razors have been around forever.'

'Neck-to-toe five o'clock shadow,' says Tom.

Lee is the only one who laughs.

Andrea decides to flag the story. She's probably got it all wrong — it's only the end that she really remembers. She was rather hoping that Tom would take over, or at least set her straight. She's astonished to think she may not have told him this story, which has stayed so long in her mind. Was she afraid he would take possession, weave Andrea's woman into some Bailey's Circus stories?

'Go on,' prompts Mary. 'She's longing to be like everyone else —'

Andrea rubs her nose. 'I'm not sure — maybe there was a change of manager. Maybe the other one left or died, or maybe it just took a long time for the freak show manager to realise he'd fallen in love with his monkey woman.' She looks around. They are with her now. 'Imagine how that would feel — he loved her despite the way she looked, so she would've known that was real love.'

They're still listening, she senses this, though their eyes are now directed at things — a bottle or bowl or overhanging branch. Andrea could almost be sitting there on her own.

'They had a proper white wedding. There was a photo. You could see her dark hair through the veil.'

Andrea remembers. The manager clasping that furry hand. Why has that image stayed in her mind so clearly? Behind the curled

192

moustache he had looked to be a handsome man. Long-legged and smiling.

'I'm hoping that wasn't the punchline,' says Bruce in a small voice. A grin begins. He hides it beneath his hand. Mumbles, 'Sorry.'

Mary giggles despite herself. 'Tell us,' she urges Andrea by way of atonement. 'We know it's not a joke. So tell us they lived happily ever after.'

Lee rolls her eyes. 'What kind of end is that?'

'A proper one,' says Mary. 'The only one I'll allow. There's too much sadness around these days.'

Lee smiles faintly. Her eyes slide away.

'Actually,' Andrea tells Mary, 'they did live happily. For something like fifteen years. They were described as a very devoted couple.'

'By who?' says Lee. 'Sorry — by *whom?*'

'By . . .' There are these moments when Andrea feels a serious resistance to being Lee's friend.

'The three-legged woman.' Tom keeps a serious face. 'And the frog man. In fact the frog man said it repeatedly.'

Lee gurgles and pushes back from the table, her chair on a tilt.

Andrea wonders if Tom has just committed an act of disloyalty.

Tom makes a frog sound.

Bruce improves on it, surprised to find he still has the knack. Bruce hasn't seen a frog since he was ten years old. For a moment he is down by his uncle's dam, eyes closed, listening and breathing in.

He has their attention.

'Wow. Can you do birds?'

'Rooster.'

'Moose? Can you —'

'No, magpie. Please?'

Bruce's mouth opens in case a magpie is waiting somewhere in his lungs. Nothing comes. Yet the croak was perfect. Best leave it at that.

'Sorry. And?' He turns to Andrea. 'Your story — '

He gets rid of the riesling by topping up Lee's and Mary's glasses.

'Doesn't matter.' Andrea smiles at them all, shaking her head. She's relieved to cast it aside. The story was starting to feel like a garage sale item: something exotic but essentially useless that no one would ever want to buy.

'Well, I want to hear it,' says Carl.

Andrea suffers a stab of impatience. *Of course* Carl would say that. He's so decent. He doesn't really want to know what became of the monkey woman; he just feels sorry for Andrea who keeps getting interrupted.

Andrea wonders how it would be to live with a man as considerate as Carl. She sneaks a glance at Mary who, off guard, looks weary. Andrea is not surprised, an entirely admirable man must be very hard to live up to.

'Did she continue to do her sideshow thing?' Carl persists.

As if he has a genuine interest. Niceness, Andrea decides, is frequently just another kind of lying. Still, she feels obliged.

'I'm not sure. I guess so; what else would she do?'

'So, no kids then?' The wine has polished Lee's vowels.

'You wouldn't want to take that risk,' says Mary. 'Well, I wouldn't. Not in her shoes.'

'What about in *hirsute*?' asks Tom in a casual voice.

Everyone laughs, including Andrea. In fact she laughs a little before she's figured out what was funny. Then she feels proud of Tom; he's clever like that — quick-witted.

'She died quite young.' Andrea's finally reached the part of the story she's sure about. 'She died, and her husband had her stuffed.'

For a moment all that can be heard is the distant hum of traffic.

'You mean stuffed as in . . . ?'

'As in stuffed,' says Bruce, and guffaws.

Andrea nods. 'As in taxidermy.'

'Gross,' says Lee.

Another silence, this time as if in respect.

Broken by Tom. 'Well,' he says 'I guess it would beat a blow-up doll.'

The others all groan or laugh, and Andrea feels a glow of pleasure that somehow she has rescued Tom, given him a chance to shine.

As the laughter dribbles to an end Lee objects. 'That's not sad, it's sick. I was expecting a love story.'

'It is,' says Mary. She reaches to touch Carl's arm. 'I think it's perfectly understandable. You just can't bear the thought of the person you love not existing.'

'But would you want it done to you?' says Tom, reaching for the pistachio nuts.

Mary glances at Carl but he's looking the other way. She smiles. 'I'd be honoured.'

Now Carl looks her. 'I'm afraid I'll have to disappoint you.'

Bruce draws the cork from the merlot brought by Carl and Mary. 'Lee wouldn't want to be stuffed. At least not by me.' He looks at his wife. 'Isn't that so, darling?'

Lee shakes her head from side to side, eyes closed, a little smile on her lips. Really, her head is saying to the rest of them, *he is too pathetic for words.*

And suddenly Andrea is pierced by dread. As if a pitchfork has been thrust into her heart. She glances at Tom, who is chewing and holding his glass out for Bruce to pour. She sees Mary's eyes move from Tom to Lee. Andrea's dread congeals into conviction.

'That wasn't the end of the story.' She hears her voice, too loud, and reins it in. 'The husband put her back in the show. People still paid to come and see her.' Andrea's gaze settles on Tom. 'She continued to be a source of income for him.'

The last sentence comes out like an accusation, and finally Andrea is able to catch Tom's eye but it tells her nothing. No attempt to either confirm or deny. Yet Andrea senses the reverberations of things falling into place. It's not as if the thought hadn't occurred; they have been spending more and more time with Lee and Bruce, arrangements that Andrea takes no part in instigating. *Keeps the boys happy*, Lee would say, and Andrea would laugh and agree.

Tom had no interest in Lee, that's what he said, rolling his eyes at the very idea. Andrea had felt a fool for asking.

Tom doesn't actually lie. He reinvents. Andrea has always understood the difference. Now she rephrases. *Tom doesn't tell the truth.*

The end of Andrea's story has brought a low moan from Mary and laughter from Bruce and Tom.

'Way to go,' says Bruce.

'He means it,' Lee says sharply, of Bruce. 'Some men like nothing better than humiliating their partners in public.'

'Oh, come on, Lee,' says Tom on Bruce's behalf.

Mary imagines Lee naked and hairy, like an Afghan hound, blinking out through a golden fringe at a shadowy crowd of faces. Then she remembers the raging, weeping, bedraggled Lee who'd camped at their place when Bruce was having it off with the real estate agent from Ashburton, and feels ashamed. It's good, thinks Mary, to see Lee back to her old self with even, surely, some added inner sparkle.

'Andrea,' asks Carl, 'why did you tell us that story?'

Andrea drags her narrowed eyes off Lee and shrugs. 'Why?'

'Because . . . maybe I'm missing the point.'

'The point,' Bruce tells Carl, 'is the same old one we hear over and over. It's a men-are-bastards story.'

'It's not.' Andrea is indignant. 'Not to me.'

196

'Then tell us, Andrea,' urges Carl. 'What do you make of that story?'

This time Andrea doesn't find Carl's manner at all insincere. This time she thinks how nice it must be to be Mary.

'I'm not sure any more,' she confesses to Carl. 'She had those years of feeling loved. He made her happy and I suppose I thought that's what matters. Once you're dead . . .'

'But he didn't love her,' says Mary. 'You couldn't exhibit someone you loved. Certainly not for profit.'

'But if she believed . . .' says Carl, for Andrea.

'Let's face it,' says Bruce, bored with all this. 'She was a poor, hairy fool.'

'He made a monkey of her.' Tom grins in Lee's direction. Andrea is watching.

'Well,' roars Mary. 'I'd a bloody sight sooner be miserable than deluded.' Just the thought has made her angry on the monkey woman's behalf.

Lee looks at Carl. *You heard what she said!* Carl moves his head a fraction. *No!* the movement says. Lee wonders what would happen if she just came out and said it anyway. She's sick of all the pretence. She'd tell Bruce like a shot but then it would all be out in the open and Carl won't have that.

'Carl and I are in love,' she would say, though Carl hasn't actually declared himself in so many words.

Of course she won't do any such thing. Lee's figured it out. The longer they can keep up the deception the more unforgivable Mary will find it. That way his wife will make the choice for him.

Lee turns to Bruce with a smile, pats his hand. 'We're behaving badly, honey. I'm sorry if you're sorry.' She can feel Carl watching.

Andrea knows that stumbling upon the monkey woman had nothing to do with chance. All this time that story has been waiting in her head. In the telling of the story lay the realisation of her own predicament. Don't be fooled, the monkey woman is saying to Andrea. Don't be a fool like I was.

'Don't think I don't know,' she blurts at Lee. 'You and Tom. You must think I'm blind.'

Lee's eyes expand and she laughs. *She laughs.* 'Me and Tom! Come on, Andrea, get a grip.' She rolls her eyes for the benefit of the others, then narrows them at Andrea. 'Whatever your husband might have told you, dearie, it's just another of his little fantasies. Surely you know that by now? Or are you the only one here who doesn't get embarrassed on his behalf?'

Andrea hears a sound like a thin taut wire snapping, but it could be just her own intake of breath. She forces herself to glance at Tom, who now sits round-shouldered, slumped and motionless — a Guy Fawke's dummy crammed into Levis and a cotton-knit shirt. He meets her look in a squinting, injured fashion. And, somehow, yes, it is her fault. Something has been severed. Things can never, now, go back to the way they have always been, the way she's used to. She has betrayed Tom. She is no better than the monkey woman's husband.

Mary wishes they hadn't come; she hates scenes. So does Carl. That look in his face when poor, insecure Andrea shrieked her accusation — he was totally shocked. Genuinely decent people quite often have an inbuilt naivity when it comes to human behaviour. Mary finds such innocence endearing, especially in a grown man.

EN ROUTE TO
DANNEVIRKE

There is a point — a place, a state of mind — between sober and drunk that Joeline has never reached. She knows it exists, the proof is all around her; it's there in their glittering eyes and their raised and reckless voices.

Joeline wants to join them, oh how she wants to join them, but previous attempts have been disastrous. One minute she's feeling bloated-but-sober and the next the room is swaying and dipping and her stomach is doing warm-up heaves that experience warns are no empty threat. Even if she stops drinking right away (and sometimes she doesn't; sometimes she forces herself to carry on regardless) she'll throw up within the next fifteen minutes. She's by-passed the good bit.

It's always the same. She never manages out of control, never needs to be carried tenderly to bed. Nothing she does warrants mention next day when that particular party is recalled/lamented/

relished in a hundred flats and bedsits.

Tonight is another chance. Tonight and green ginger wine. She'll drink the whole bottle if need be. Provided, that is, she doesn't leave it unguarded and Fritz isn't passing his carefully mixed vodka and orange to every girl within arm's reach. Carmen will stick with her Johnnie Walker, raising the battered silver flask to her mouth with an air of tragic bravado. Carmen is good at feisty-yet-fragile. Men fall at her feet.

Joeline hasn't sighted Carmen since they arrived. She will be somewhere pivotal, doing something people will talk about. Carmen herself will talk about it. A different kind of drinker might claim not to remember (Did I do that? Oh God, did I really?) but Carmen always has total recall. (I wanted to know how it felt. I thought, bloody hell, why not? You know how it is.)

Joeline doesn't. She fears she may never, ever, know how it is. She might end up married and living in Dannevirke with nothing even to look back on. That kind of thing happens to girls who can never cut loose from their own common sense. The whole point of drinking is to become a person you wouldn't approve of. Bloated and vomiting both fall well short of a character change. Tonight and green ginger wine may be Joeline's last chance.

'Can I nibble your neck?' A voice at her ear. Joeline slaps a protective hand in place before even turning her head. This is how hopeless she is. Okay, he has fat pink cheeks and thin beige hair, but had she reached that blessed state of drunkenness she might have allowed him to nibble regardless. And then gone off to find a neck of her own choosing.

She seems to have been in this place forever, clutching her bottle, stepping this way and that to let people pass, avoiding eyes that might slide into hers.

Fritz is making his way towards her. His round face comes and goes like a river winding through hill country. He's towing a girl with fuzzy red hair and a tight purple shirt. When he has Joeline clearly in view he shouts out to her but his words are smothered by voices and the patient throb of a bass guitar. Joeline takes a large gulp of ginger wine in case that's what brings him her way.

Now he shouts in her ear. 'This is Liz. Tell her how nice I am.'

'He is,' Joeline hollers. 'Fritz is lovely. We work together.'

'She's Joeline,' shouts Fritz into the girl's fine, fluffy hair. 'At parties I point out the beautiful woman and Joeline goes up and says, "My friend really likes you."'

Liz looks bemused. She flashes a vague smile, then grabs Fritz's hand and tugs him away. As Fritz squeezes past her Joeline asks him if he's seen Carmen. Fritz points at a torn poster of Fidel Castro, or perhaps the wall. 'She's taking her clothes off.'

Joeline is torn between good-grief and why-can't-it-be-me. She begins burrowing her way in Castro's direction. It's a matter of finding a niche between bodies and shoving a little. Some people object but most will shuffle aside. Someone spills beer on her shoulder. A young woman smiles and says, 'Hey there,' but Joeline can't place her. Jerry Lee Lewis is skiing on piano keys. Joeline reaches the wall and sees to her right the curved mouldings of a doorway.

She waits while two over-excited young men — the rugby-playing kind — push their way through from the other direction.

'With everyone looking?'

Joeline strains to hear.

'No one was looking. Only me.'

'And they were actually . . .'

'Bloody oath they were.'

More beer has spilt: she can feel it soaking through to her arm. She wants to grab hold of the nearest of the rugby men and demand some details. Like — describe the woman. If there was room to raise the green ginger bottle she'd take another swig. Carmen or not,

Joeline wishes she'd seen. Something like that could jolt you from sober into the region of uncontrol.

In this room the music is louder and red gauze dims and tints the lighting. Somewhere there is a record player. A cluster of people are dancing, but in an odd, almost motionless way. Their heads are all turned in the direction of the curtainless windows. Beyond which a tree — possibly quince — flickers palely. Joeline edges forward and now sees Carmen.

This is a big old house with long, low windows and sills wide enough to comfortably sit on, but Carmen is standing. She has removed her stretchy shirt and her black lacy bra and is jiggling around to 'Great Balls of Fire'. Her eyes are closed as if this is a private moment: just her and Jerry Lee Lewis. She does not see, as Joeline now does, the rolling eyes of her female audience or the glee-fully slack jaws of the males. Joeline takes a very large gulp of her wine.

'May I?' says a woman in a fringed crimson shawl. She lifts the bottle from Joeline's fingers, helping herself. Joeline doesn't care; her eyes are glued on Carmen's bouncing pink-tipped breasts.

The song skids to an end and Carmen opens her eyes in the manner of a startled deer. A man in a tiger-striped jerkin reaches towards her with a glass — a proper stemmed goblet — of what may be champagne. As she leans out to take it each of Carmen's pale and perfect breasts extends like the centrepiece of an ornate ceiling rose.

Joeline feels neither awe nor envy. There is no time, for the room is swaying. Once again she has gone too far and missed the station. Maybe if she lies down now the train will kindly shunt back and allow her to leap gaily onto the platform signposted *Abandon*.

She reaches the passage where people sit and lie on the greasy carpet. She tries the nearest door. 'Do you mind? Oh, hi.'

It's Fritz's redhead.

'Sorry,' says Joeline. 'Looking for a bedroom.' But she stays there a moment, gawping, for this is the biggest bathroom she's ever seen. Ugly sea-green walls with glimpses of yellow beneath the brushstrokes, ripped linoleum, a bright naked bulb dangling, and directly beneath it, perched like an eagle in a desert, a big yellowed bathtub. Liz fastens her belt and stares at Joeline via the mottled mirror that hangs above the ancient handbasin.

Joeline closes that door and picks her way to the next one. 'Get out.' Two voices in unison; then there is giggling. She crosses the hall. No voice from within and the light switch works. A double bed covered in duffel coats and a couple of raggedy furs. Joeline clears a space and lies down. There's a light cord hanging just within reach and she pulls it.

In darkness this house is the inter-island ferry. Despite herself Joeline thinks cafeteria, can smell sad pies and cheese withering on toast. Mentally, she propels herself outside and now stands clutching a rail. The wind slices her hair and next to her arm is a rough grey sleeve. Its owner smells smokey and male but she doesn't look. Instead she closes her eyes and tries to remember what she has eaten, this way to eliminate surprises. Once there was a small black circle she has never been able to account for. She tries to calculate how many steps to the bathroom if or when the need arises.

The door opens. Joeline's eyes screw tight against the prospect of light; even so, she can tell when it doesn't come. In the dark someone is beside the bed shovelling the duffel coats on top of Joeline. She guesses it's Carmen. They've flatted together for six months now, enough time to develop an instinct.

'Car?'

'Ah,' murmurs Carmen, 'that's where you got to. I think I just made a right fool of myself.' She giggles.

Joeline cautiously raises her head. Some of the coats slide onto the floor. 'I know. I saw you.' There's a swell and she's back out on deck clutching the rail. 'I might throw up. Were you looking for me?'

'Not exactly.' Carmen eases herself down beside Joeline and the wirewove goes with her. Joeline braces herself against sliding down, against the inevitable colliding of flesh, though this is her friend and it shouldn't matter. The ginger wine has failed Joeline badly.

A sliver of light as the door opens. 'You in here?' It's a male voice: the private-school kind.

Carmen speaks to the ceiling. 'I'm looking after my friend; she's not very well.'

He turns on the light. It's the tiger-striped jerkin.

'Oh, that's no good,' he says, gliding towards them. 'No good at all.' He looks down at Carmen in the ditch, then at Joeline half covered in coats and clutching the headboard. 'Merlin,' he says, bobbing about, light on his feet. His hair spills down over his shoulders. It's greying in front and could do with a wash.

'Joeline — Merlin,' says Carmen in a wooden voice. 'It's not his real name.'

He jabs a theatrical finger. 'That's your assumption.'

Joeline closes her eyes to make them both to go away. The bed lurches. Merlin has got up there in one step as if it was a verandah. Joeline opens her eyes fractionally so she can see him balanced up there above them. 'This light is far too bright,' he says, and whips from his trouser pocket a flicker of blue fabric. He leans out further than balance should allow and drapes the plastic lightshade. The room turns a magical blue. Merlin repositions himself, every movement a giant wave of the ocean, but Joeline is finding her sea legs. She looks down at Carmen, who is now fully clothed and propped on one elbow.

Merlin positions himself cross-legged on the end of the bed, facing them both. He has something in his hand.

'Have you lovely ladies ever been hypnotised?'

Carmen laughs, Joeline shakes her head. Merlin raises a hand and lets a cord tumble from it — a cord attached to large gold disk. He clears his throat and speaks in a lowered, husky voice. 'Gaze on this golden orb: it is the sun. Watch it closely and you will feel the warmth it transmits, a warmth that soothes.'

Joeline can feel that warmth, she's sure she can. It burns in her cheeks.

'You are on a beach. Beneath you is warm sand. Feel the sand. Listen to the waves. They pound, they hiss.'

Joeline holds her breath, the better to concentrate, but she can only hear laughter, voices, the thumping of feet and the throb of drums. Somewhere beneath all that there are surely waves. She strains to hear them.

'Watch the sun,' prompts Merlin.

The sun swings back and forth, back and forth, back and forth. The man beyond the sun says Joeline is feeling sleepy and maybe she is; she hopes she is. She must not fail at this, for isn't it what she's been seeking? That the timid, judgemental part of her brain will shut down, even just for one night? She must not find this situation ridiculous. Must not find, must not find, must not find.

'Your limbs are heavy; you are sliding into the land of sleep.'

She needs more time. Ought she say so, or will the act of speaking undo the progress she may have already made? She should be too tired to even open her mouth. *She must try harder.*

It's too late. Merlin is leaning forward, moving his hand in front of Carmen's impassive face, her wide unblinking eyes. He smiles and looks at Joeline. She imagines her own face to be mask-like. Maybe it's worked and she's already under? You can't know when you're hypnotised. That's the whole point. If people knew, they wouldn't get up on stage and act like they were in a bath or a southerly gale, or were hens or rabbits.

205

Merlin is staring hard at Joeline. She can't keep it up. She blinks, shakes her head apologetically.

'You're blocking,' he says. 'Some people do that. They're afraid to let go.'

Joeline nods. It's weird, as if he can see inside her. 'Sorry,' she whispers, but his attention is now on Carmen.

'Carmen,' he says, and his voice has returned to normal. 'Carmen, I want you to sit up.'

Carmen sits up. Her face is doll-like, vacant.

'Now I want you to get on your hands and knees.'

'What are you going to do?' The question's asked before Joeline has even given it thought. She's not sure if she's concerned or just curious, but she sees Carmen's mouth quiver briefly as if repressing a smile.

'You can't make people do something under hypnosis that they wouldn't normally do.' Merlin's voice has a sharpish edge.

'I know that's what people say.' Joeline shovels the remaining coats to the foot of the bed.

'Well, it's true,' says Merlin impatiently. 'Carmen,' he says. 'Carmen, your friend is going soon. Why don't you hug her goodbye?'

Carmen sits back on her heels, twists around and clasps Joeline in a big warm hug. Joeline hugs back and is pleased by her own ready response. She can't see Carmen's face.

'Bye, Joeline,' says Carmen, releasing her hold. Her voice sounds odd. 'See you later.'

'Okay,' says Joeline uncertainly. She doesn't want to go, not yet. This isn't because she's concerned for Carmen but because she wants Merlin to try again. To leave is to be condemned to caution.

But Carmen has dismissed her. It may all be an act. That possibility cannot be ruled out. Carmen may have come to the bedroom knowing that Merlin would follow. At any moment she could burst out laughing. Perhaps this will happen when Joeline has left. Perhaps the two of them planned the whole thing as a way of getting the room to themselves. All Joeline knows for sure is that they both want her to go, so what else can she do?

The floor is steady beneath her feet as she walks to the door. She's aware, now, of how noisy it is outside this room, and how silent inside it. And suddenly she wants to be out there among the noise and the crowd, can't get there fast enough. Could this mean she is acting under instruction? If she is, in fact, *under*, who will snap her out of it? At the doorway she turns back but Merlin and Carmen are stroking each other, mutually mesmerised.

In the passage Joeline steps around and over bodies and bottles. Her stomach has settled. She feels entirely, dismally, sober. She tries to recall when and where she last saw her ginger wine. She decides she will look for the bottle or, failing that, Fritz and the uncomplicated comfort of friendship. Just as soon as she's had a pee.

There's a girl at the door of the bathroom waiting and jiggling, but not for long. 'Oh, bugger this.' As she leaves she bumps into Joeline, surely on purpose, and glares. 'Ooops,' says Joeline automatically. 'Sorry.'

She takes the girl's place at the door and almost at once hears a promising clanking and gurgling. A man comes out. He has a long beakish nose and one arm in a sling and Joeline thinks of a stork bringing a baby. 'Sorry,' he says. 'I'd wait a bit if I were you.'

Joeline doesn't wait. She takes a deep breath and holds it for as long as she can. The cistern is still groaning and clanging. It's up by the ceiling, the kind with a rope that should end in a handle, though this one offers only a small, fraying knot. The wooden seat has a sharp-edged split. Joeline raises it up and squats over the bowl. The water is still rushing and churning.

Joeline once went on a school trip to a hydro dam. They all stood behind the barrier fence watching as the water was released. It was the fiercest thing Joeline has ever seen. Above the sonic din the teacher was shouting about cubic capacity and megawattage but all Joeline could think of was being part of that glorious turmoil; the urge to scramble over the fence and jump was intense.

The door opens and a young man comes in. Joeline is squeaking, 'Sorry . . . occupied . . . excuse me . . .' but he takes no notice. He pushes the door shut behind him and smiles in her direction.

'Good evening,' he says. 'How are you?'

He can't want to know this. She's never seen him before. She's crouching here with her almost-new Levis concertinaed around her knees and he's acting like they're already aquainted. He sniffs.

'I'm sure that pong wasn't you,' he says kindly. 'I'm in a terrible hurry.' He presses his thighs together and gives a kind of two-legged hop in Joeline's direction.

'Too bad,' says Joeline. 'You'll just have to wait.' She means out there in the passage. The flushing has finished and the sound of her urine trickling into the bowl seems to be magnified ten times over. This room is a soundshell.

'I can't,' says the young man. 'Sorry, but I can't.' He's very definite and doesn't seem in the least distressed. Now he's unzipping himself.

'You could use the bath, I guess.'

'Hardly. It's not connected. Look. The water just runs onto the floor.'

She sees this is true. Taps but no downpipe. 'How odd.'

'Girls take so long,' he complains, shuffling in close behind her left shoulder. 'Just move forward a fraction. I have perfect aim.'

Joeline jerks forward with repugnance and braces herself. She hears his trickle join hers.

'There,' he says, 'what did I tell you?'

She looks up and he's smiling down at her. She likes his smile and she likes his slanting green eyes.

'I'm Callum,' he says, 'and if you want paper I'm afraid there doesn't seem to be any.'

Joeline laughs. 'I don't dare risk moving until you've finished, so you will let me know?'

'If you tell me your name.'

'I'm Joeline,' she says. She's about to add *and I'm horribly sober*, but suddenly it doesn't seem to matter.

ON TV

4.00 Jed and Harriet have a delivery problem.

'When she be here?' says Jed once again. Not, this time, to his mother, whose turned-down mouth tells him her patience is stretched. Instead he speaks to the window, so close that his breath leaves a faint mist on the pane. In this mist he draws a square. Then adds four legs, though these remain invisible until he delivers a second breath and then they appear, as he knew they would. It disappoints him that this trick works every time. Magic should be unreliable.

'I'm waiting,' he says through the glass to the driveway where the car would already be if anyone cared. Jed wants a world where everyone does what they said they would do and does it on time. He screws up his eyes in an effort to make the car appear between himself and the fence. A greenish, brownish car with scratches and dings and an inside that smells like a puddle of water. A car of no interest except that Jed and Harriet sometimes get to ride in it and today it is bringing them everything Jed has been missing out on.

'How big?'

Her look says he's asked that already.

'This big or *thaaaat* big?' Stretching his arms out and staggering beneath the invisible weight.

It works. The edges of her mouth strain to go up, though she's trying to stop them.

Plays me like a violin, thinks Harriet. *No, not a violin, something you pluck at — a mandolin perhaps, or a balalaika.* Each single note resounding in her cavities: chest, womb, throat, eye sockets. How can someone so small be so cunning?

He has old eyes. A number of people have said so. At the Three Lamps end of Ponsonby Road a woman in a leopardskin hat had looked into the pram and said, 'This one has made many journeys.'

And only last week, watching Jed bury a matchbox full of dead flies, Ginny had said, 'That boy's been through some heavy shit in one of his past lives.' Harriet had stifled a groan. She'd hoped all that stuff had been left behind her in the city where it belonged.

Nevertheless, there are moments when Harriet watches her son and wishes she'd never seen *E.T.* There wasn't much about Jed's father, Hughie, that was arguably terrestrial. Nothing that would, for certain, connect him to this planet.

And now Ginny, who she'd thought of as being as sharp and down to earth as a spade.

Is it that Harriet attracts weirdness? Twelve thousand people in this town and Harriet chums up with Ginny, who should've been here by now but may just have forgotten. Or have been waylaid by unfinished business from one of her past lives. Harriet allows herself a grin at Ginny's expense.

'Pingu,' cheeps Jed, still at the window. 'Pingu. Pingu. Pingu. Pingu . . .'

It's a competition. If she admits to irritation he will have won. Harriet remembers the company of adults, weird or otherwise. The kindness, the tact, the lack of repetition.

'Pingu . . . Pingu . . . Pingu.' He is winding down, or perhaps just giving her false hope. *Pingu* the penguin is on every afternoon, before *Teletubbies*. Jed watches both on those glorious days when he is invited after playgroup to the home of his friend Charlton. Harriet goes too, like a handmaiden or personal secretary. She sits at the kitchen table drinking instant coffee with Charlton's mother, Lisa, and sometimes also with Charlton's grandmother, Laura.

Harriet isn't entirely comfortable with these friends that Jed has thrust upon her. Lisa is very young and her mother seems . . . *smug* is the word that offers itself but Harriet sets it aside and chooses *provincial*. Which cannot be a criticism since people like Lisa and Laura, who — unlike Ginny — belong in this place, are the kind of people Harriet wants Jed to grow up among. *Real* people, she'd called them when she made that decision.

Poor Jed. Already the children's programmes are over, and those are all she plans to allow him to watch. It's important to mark clear boundaries. They will both be bound by rules. In this house there will be no mindless channel-surfing. Programmes will be selected in advance. To this end Harriet has bought a *Listener* — in fact she has bought two, although she could probably have gauged tonight's programme from the following Friday's and put the extra $3.20 towards the next power bill.

Jed lived in channel-surfing houses for his first two and a half years, but seems already not to remember. Rather to Harriet's relief: it's impossible to monitor the programmes — the fragments of programmes — watched when it's someone else's TV.

Then came the months with just the two of them in an ugly overpriced unit. They went out a lot, for obvious reasons, to the playground, or visiting Harriet's friends. There was no need for TV.

Harriet had thought it would be the same here. She doesn't believe in all that grabbing at things you don't really need and can't afford.

She wasn't aware that she was depriving her son. Even when she'd stood down the back of the cluttered shop staring at the dead black screen jammed between the vacuum cleaners and a tangle of skis, she'd thought just of herself. Had imagined the relief it would surely be to have Jed's attention diverted away in programme-length chunks. Seen herself curled with a book and a mug of tea. Or, better still, taking a bath.

She'd envisaged Jed on his belly, the way he lies at Charlton's place, with Charlton, who is several months younger, sprawled in carefully observed imitation. Chins propped, eyes fixed, mouths open. That last was the bit that excited Harriet — Jed's mouth gaping and, for considerable stretches of time, *motionless*.

An extra $18, the man had told her, to have it delivered. He said this after she'd been up the street to the eftpos machine and returned clutching the price of the TV and a slip of paper saying her balance was now $3.65. She told the man she'd arrange to collect the set tomorrow.

On the walk home from playgroup she told Jed. She knew he'd be pleased but she wasn't prepared for deliriously ecstatic. 'Our TV,' he shrieked over and over, running, skipping, laughing all the way along Gordon Street. 'Our TV. Our *Pingu*. Our *Teletubbies*.'

They'd detoured to walk past Ginny's place but no one was home. 'No big truck,' said Jed, but was unable to manage his customary disappointment. Once, when they'd called on Ginny and Mac was home he'd swung Jed up into the passenger seat and driven around the block.

Harriet rang Ginny that night. No problem, said Ginny. She'd pick the set up in the morning.

Jed has been waiting, now, twenty-nine hours. It isn't fair. 'Where is she?' he asks the ceiling. 'What she doing?'

Harriet hates to nag when it's a favour and everything, but she rings anyway and after quite a long time Mac answers. Not Mac himself but his voice saying in a dopey American accent, 'Little Ginny and Big Mac are missing you already. Y'all just leave us a message after the beep.'

So Harriet rings the man at Good Deal Traders, who tells her a girl with a ring in her nose came and got the TV some time after lunch. 'Now you're gonna tell me there's a problem with that?'

'No,' says Harriet bleakly. 'No problem.'

In the *Listener* she looks up what they could be watching right now, '*Justine and Susie squabble over Tom and Fisher learns a secret . . . Marcus whips up some guacamole . . . What's on at the movies . . . The Huxtable family prepares for Theo's graduation . . .*' For a moment Harriet feels as bereft as her son; the unaccessed airwaves are full of people she's missing out on.

5.30 Ginny feels sure she's on a roll.
When Ginny ran into Corin outside Video Hire he claimed he'd summoned her there by transmitting beams of intelligence.

'Intelligence?' Ginny queried. 'I'll buy the transmitting, but intelligence?' She saw the uncertainty of his smile and felt ashamed of herself. 'Testosterone,' she invented quickly. 'You're transmitting testosterone, babe.' Then she wet her lips with her studded tongue, because he liked to think she was dangerous.

His smile settled in then, narrow-eyed and knowing. Not at all a Corin smile. He's been practising, thought Ginny, and she imagined him at his blue-rimmed shaving mirror teaching a magnified mouth to leer.

'Actually,' she said, 'I was looking for you.'

His hands kept inching towards her, though they knew that touching wasn't allowed, not in High Street and especially not on a busy Friday afternoon.

'It's been five days!' Corin bleated, close to her ear. At the same time a woman stepped out of the pharmacy next door to the video shop and said, 'Corin, dear, how's your mum? And Diane? Tell Janet I haven't forgotten about the pink chrysanths.' And Ginny had smirked up at a poster of Harrison Ford with his tie unknotted, as if she trying to decide what she wanted to watch, while Corin was mumbling fine, thanks, fine, right, and smiling like the nice boy he didn't want to be.

But Ginny was also replaying Corin's voice, so full of indignation and blame. *Five days!* She pressed her forearm against her inside pocket to be sure the money was still there, crisply folded. Her decision was made. The idea had come to her just like that and her instincts, today, are in very good form.

Earlier, heading back from Good Deal Traders, she'd detoured past the old pub telling herself just the $10 she had in her pocket — just that and no more. Ten dollars and — why not? — one rum and cola, and then she would leave.

But she had to use her eftpos card for the drink and it's economic to take out some cash when you make a purchase, that's what they say, so she did.

And when the pile of twenties was gone Ginny had a feeling, a very strong feeling, that she'd been *almost there*. It was like when you're searching for someone who's maybe been taken hostage and you try all these houses but none is the right house. And then you go in a gate and up a path and you get this feeling. You just know that this is going to be the one.

So she asked for ten twenty-cent pieces — which really didn't count because $2 was next to nothing — and fed them into the machine. She'd always felt that this particular machine was well inclined towards her, though it had so far, shown her no favour.

Three coins played was all it needed. The machine sang its song and the coins came tumbling out in such numbers that Sandy rushed in from the bar with an empty glass tankard to catch the spillage. Only then did Ginny notice her company. Some old geezer in a Rasta beanie, Guppy Brown and a handicapped woman. It didn't seem proper, somehow, for a middle-aged woman in a wheelchair to sit in a pub playing the machines.

Sandy weighed the coins. Two hundred dollars. The old geezer clapped and Guppy raised his fist and shook it, presumably on Ginny's behalf.

Ginny had spun the Cortina around and driven back through town. Parked out the back of Paper Plus. She was trying to remember things she wanted but never had the money to buy. Must be hundreds, but not one came to mind. Something for Mac then? But Mac hated her playing the machines and he'd want to know where she got the money.

So Corin, then. Corin had no problem about the machines — in fact that's how they met. He had told her later he had chosen the one next to her on purpose. Corin liked her skinny, foxy looks. He liked the stud in her tongue and the rings in her nose. Admiration was hard to resist and, besides, there were things they had in common, like too much time on their hands.

You could say that was Mac's fault for being on the road for days and nights at a time. Plus, Ginny was wary of making friends because of being on the benefit and you never know who you could trust. In a town like this everyone has a cousin or mother or aunt working for Income Support, and Ginny had signed the form to say she was just Mac's boarder, someone to look after the place and feed the cat when he was away. One stray word about where she slept and they wouldn't just stop her benefit, they'd expect her to pay it back. A whole two years' worth. Thousands and thousands of dollars.

And if there was one thing Ginny was always good at it was making friends. *Linking with people*, they used to call it when she was going to Group. 'You have a real talent for linking with people, Ginny.'

You were supposed to find positive stuff to say at the beginning, and again at the end, since the last words were the ones people usually remembered. So there may have been other good qualities that they mentioned, but. *linking* was the one that Ginny remembered.

She'd linked with Mac the day he stopped his truck just north of Bulls to give her a lift. And she'd linked with Ashmita and Joe at the local dairy. And she'd linked with Harriet, who could be trusted since she was also on the benefit and knew how it was for a woman.

And she'd definitely linked with Corin.

'Follow me,' Ginny told him, then walked up the street towards Paper Plus with Corin a couple of metres behind. She walked through the shop and out the back door to the council's wildly optimistic carpark. So much space and so few cars that each time she parks there it makes her grin. Corin had got waylaid by someone between stationery and the Easter bunnies. He has lived in this town all his life.

Now, while she waits in the car, Ginny tries to imagine how it must feel to have so many linkages in place before you were even born.

Trapped, is how it must feel.

When Corin climbs in beside her she shows him her winnings. 'Got anything planned for tonight, babe?'

'Like what?'

'Motel.' She watches his eyes expand.

'He's away?'

'No. Well, he is, but he'll be back later on.'

'So, just for an hour or something?' He's disappointed.

'Don't be tacky. I mean all night.'

'Yeah? Really? So — you've told him . . . 'bout us?'

Ginny sighs and shakes her head. They've been through this before. At first Corin was wildly happy just to have got what he wanted, but now he objects to sharing. A small part of her is flattered but it's a very small part.

'But he'll know,' Corin insists. 'If you're away all night. He might not be very smart but I think he'll manage to figure that out.'

Ginny is offended on Mac's behalf. 'Actually he's a whole lot smarter than you, and he's an adult. And he earns a living.'

Corin is grinning as if somehow this puts him ahead on points. 'So what's gonna happen? He finds out and then what? I mean, is this some kind of game?'

Ginny doesn't answer. She sees no need. Instincts cannot be expected to explain themselves and hers are not on trial here. But if they were, her bones would defend them. Sometimes, her bones would say, *you just have to chuck the cat among the pigeons or the flaming aerosol can into the henhouse.*

6.00 Mac calls home.

At that sentimental stretch of road just outside Bulls Mac allows himself to ring home. He limits his calls but it's still a shock each month when the bill comes. Sometimes he'll hold off ringing until he's almost there, maybe fifteen minutes away. But then he hits the town belt and the bad years after Beverley left come back and have him grabbing for his mobile. Those days when the closer Mac got to home the colder and deader he would feel.

She used to complain — Beverley — that he took her for granted, and Mac won't be making that mistake again. Too many calls are costly but too few would be false economy. There's a delicate balance, which Mac hopes he's achieving. In Beverley's time there were no cellphones or it could've made all the difference.

Mac gets himself on the answerphone and has to chuckle. He doesn't bother about a message. She'll have just nipped up to the dairy for smokes. She likes to make out she's quit but he knows she hasn't. He can feel the grin still hanging around on his face. These coming-home calls always make him feel like an astronaut who's worried that, in his absence, earth may have changed orbit, or even galaxies.

6.30 Ginny follows her instincts.

Corin has never before stayed in a motel. Ginny finds this remarkable. It's twelve years since she was nineteen but, as far as she remembers, she had at that age done almost everything it was possible to do. His delight peeves her.

'I've stayed in much better places than this,' she tells him as he empties sachets of coffee into the white cups he has carefully placed in their saucers. He makes no response. He may not have even heard her above the racing cars that scream at them from the over-coloured screen.

They'd driven around considering possibilities. Ginny had in mind Camellia Lodge because of the windows that were criss-crossed into diamonds in a Shakespearian way. But the sign at the lodge said No Vacancy, and this one, at least from the outside, had looked new and rather important. In the interests of discretion they'd driven on past and left the Cortina under the big tree behind the picnic table at the reserve, where they used to sometimes go when the days were longer and warmer.

Corin had kept out of sight while Ginny booked in; he was worried about being recognised and word getting back to his parents, and anyway, why pay for two if you don't need to?

Ginny said she was Andrea Horne, a name she'd used once or twice in the past. She wrote her address as 15 Hakanoa St, Herne Bay, Auckland. She'd lived for a while near Hakanoa Street and had liked the name.

'A friend will be calling later to drop off my gear,' Ginny said, and the face of the woman behind the counter took on an unconvincingly inscrutable look that said, *it's-none-of-my-business-but-don't-think-I'm-fooled.*

Maureen Claridge said the name on her lapel. She put on glasses to study Ginny's immaculate writing.

'Do you know, Andrea, that you have a double in this town? I've seen her a couple of times at McGregor's Garage.'

'My sister,' said Ginny, waving her hands to show that life's little coincidences never failed to delight her. 'Everyone says we're peas in a pod.' She pulled the notes out of her pocket, getting in first. 'I expect to be leaving early so best I pay you now.' Seeing the little glow of relief as the key was handed over. Unit seven. Seven was one of Ginny's lucky numbers.

Watching Corin spoon sugar into their cups Ginny thinks, for a moment, of Mac at the kitchen bench boiling and pouring. Mac who wants a big rig and a couple of sprogs and Ginny at the stove stirring the rice risotto. A great furry spider binding her up in his dreams.

Corin sets the cups on the bedside table and lies down next to Ginny. The bed is vast: a prairie of possibilities. Up until now they've made do with the confines of the Cortina or the remarkable squalor of Corin's sleepout. This second option entails creeping like robbers between heavily scented roses and parental windows. Ginny wouldn't take her lover to Mac's place, despite what he's going to think. She does have scruples.

Corin's arm runs across Ginny's thighs. *All night*, she thinks. The prospect tastes like peppermint cremes. In the morning light he will see that her bones show and her neck has more skin than required. He will feel, if not revulsion, at least a tremor of distaste.

Smiling, she turns her body to align with his and gropes for his hand. The channel is changed: Iraq is the cause of growing concern. Corin's hand is exploring possibilities other than Ginny. He has a

TV in the sleepout, but a fourteen-inch screen and only three channels. No continuous sport, no uninterrupted movies.

Ginny remembers the TV in the boot of her car. Ooops, she thinks. Sorry, Harriet. But what difference can one night make?

'I'm starving,' says Corin. 'When are we gonna eat?'

7.30 Harriet succumbs to self-pity.

'I'm really pissed off,' says Harriet to the bathroom taps. She finds that she does this quite often — converses with household utensils and fittings. Is that a cause for concern?

If she'd known that Ginny wouldn't turn up before dark, Harriet and Jed could have walked into town. Maybe gone to McDonald's to share a sundae. Something to keep his impatience at bay.

While Jed is having his bath she presses redial and the real Mac answers on the very first ring. Harriet asks to speak to Ginny.

'I thought you were going to be her,' Mac says. He's only just got in and no sign, no note.

'She can't have gone far,' says Harriet.

If she sounds snappish Mac doesn't seem to notice. He seems, in fact reassured. He'll take a stroll up town — bound to find Ginny there being led astray. Should he give her a message?

'Tell her I rang.' Harriet is needing to keep it brief. Even with the phone cord fully extended she can only just see the tap end of the bath and half a blue duck.

'Sure thing,' says Mac, his confidence clearly restored and so contagious that Harriet lets Jed stay up way past his bedtime playing Snap.

Now Harriet sits on the edge of her son's bed and reads aloud, but she's aware of both of them listening to every passing vehicle. She's aware, too, of what a small family unit they are, she and Jed.

When one book is finished he hands her another and she reads

221

that too. Her voice is a bulwark against the night, against the urge to ring her sister in Oamaru or one of her flaky friends in Auckland just for the feeling of being connected to something and someone. An adult.

'Ginny might be home,' offers Jed. 'She might be home now.'

So Harriet rings again, but there's only Mac's silly cowpoke voice. He has evidently found Ginny and now they will be eating at the café. A couple. Free to spend a Friday night however they please.

Harriet's envy appals her. She has a sweet-smelling son with bristling hair and a scab on his nose. Who could need more?

In the absence of lollies she mixes cocoa and sugar in the bottom of a mug and takes it to him.

8.00 Mac has growing cause for concern.

Mac goes straight to the Central Hotel. Which once really was, but the town has grown, like a plant, towards the sun and the Central is now at the south end. It has Mac's respect for having largely resisted fashion. Except, that is, for the regrettable refurbishment of the former office as 'The Casino Room', as dim and glitteringly icon-filled as any cathedral.

Mac had reckoned on finding Ginny there among the sacramental losers. Near enough rubbing shoulders yet oblivious to one another, their concentration so private and intense — like each of them is perched in a cubicle crapping.

He does the circuit: Cora Petrie, Davey Collins, Guppy Brown and no one at the other machines. None of them even looks up, and Mac is on his way out when Guppy speaks.

'Mac, the man. Bet you're gonna get a slap up-meal tonight.' Then he shoots a hand over his mouth. 'She hasn't told you. Be a surprise. I din say a word, okay?'

His neighbours look up.

'Yeah. She's a good little one, your missus,' says Davey Collins.

'One out of the box,' endorses Cora.

'Right,' says Mac agreeably. Ginny the hero. Someone wins and it's like an *achievement* — that person's beaten the odds, proved that winning is possible. They don't even have the nous, this lot, to feel envious.

She's smarter than them so why does she do it?

Mac walks along High Street peering into cafés and bars. He wishes he'd brought his phone; she's probably home by now. And pleased with herself. Mac doesn't approve but he does like to see her happy. He turns for home, his legs in a hurry, strides so big he could be skating.

There's a call on his answerphone. Constable Shane McKinnon, and would Mac give him a ring. Mac's fingers shake a little on the dial buttons but Shane sounds relaxed. 'Evening, Mac. Would you be missing a Ford Cortina?'

Mac thinks of the car he passed yesterday, curled in on itself like a foetus. Policemen and firemen doing their thing, though, as always, he'd barely glanced. Stuff like that on your mind could be asking for trouble. Shane's still waiting.

'What is it?' Mac blurts.

'No panic,' says the cop. 'It's parked in the reserve, kind of hidden away. Know anything about a TV set? Like, has yours gone missing?'

Mac has to check in case he'd walked right past an empty space. But it's there the same as it was two days ago when he left. 'No, it's here.'

'And your car. You knew it was there?'

'No. My . . . friend uses it, but she's . . . You think the car was nicked?'

'What d'*you* reckon. TV in the boot. Your boot doesn't seem to lock, by the way.'

'No,' says Mac. 'Never did.'

8.30 Maureen's suspicions may be confirmed and Lisa is discontented.

'That's her in seven.' Maureen holds the curtain aside so that Lisa can peer, balancing plates. 'And there's a chap. Staying the night you can bet, only she didn't bother to mention.'

Lisa waits until the woman, dangling plastic bags, triggers the intruder lights. 'Yeah, I know her. Drives around in an old Cortina. Jenny someone.'

'I knew,' says Maureen with satisfaction. She lets the curtain fall. 'Sister my eyebrow.'

'She's been here maybe a couple of years. That's definitely her. She gets round a bit with . . . you've seen that little fulla Jed that Charlton likes so much? Well, his mum is friends with this one.'

Maureen follows Lisa into the kitchen. 'Takes all sorts,' she says, opening the big fridge, 'but she doesn't look much chop to me.'

Lisa grins down at the dishes she's scraping. *Doesn't look much cop.* She can take Maureen off to perfection saying that sort of stuff. But this time Lisa feels inclined to agree. She's seen that woman with Harriet, the two of them all palsy-walsy. Maybe because they're about the same age — older than her. But what does age count? Lisa's friends, the ones her age who are still around (and that in itself says something about them), they all seem like kids.

It's not easy to make new friends when you still live at home with a mother who really should take a good look at herself. Who thinks she's Tina bloody Turner, spilling out the top of her dresses and flashing her thighs. When the fact is that, unleashed from their pantihose, the flesh on those thighs looks like custard that's been baked on a tilt.

'I can find out for sure, if you want,' she tells Maureen. 'Would just take a call.'

Maureen nods towards the dining room. 'When you've finished in there.'

8.45 Ginny is feeling a trifle shortchanged.

Ginny studies her Junior Whopper, which is the size and shape of a powder compact. She holds it up on the palm of her hand.

'Are we talking junior mouse or junior ant?'

But Corin just throws her a tender smile. He's intent on unpacking his Double Whopper Meal (with fries and a drink of your choice) without missing any crucial action at Hamilton's Rugby Park, where the Chiefs are playing the Auckland Blues.

Ginny had been the one to walk alone to McDonald's and the bottle store because the match had already started and was of no interest to her. Luckily there had been time to use the motel bed in the manner to which it was accustomed before the game kicked off. All the same, there's a lot of night still to go and Ginny finds herself wondering about her chances of a partial refund if they leave right now.

9.00 Mac fears the worst.

Shane McKinnon pops around to pick up Mac and his spare key just as soon as the sergeant gets back from his dinner. Shane's wife Michelle is the cousin of Mac's ex-wife Beverley, and this makes for a little awkwardness between the two men.

There is, Shane insists, no cause for worry. If a woman was in some kind of trouble why would she bother to lock the car?

Mac has no answer to that, but he finds the question less than reassuring. He doesn't want to argue with the law, but his own — unspoken — reasoning goes: if you steal a car to carry your stolen TV, why would you lock the car but leave the TV in the boot that didn't lock?

It's not like the big city, Shane says, sounding relaxed and knowledgeable. Here it comes down to just a handful of youngsters with too much time on their hands.

'Mind you,' he adds. 'I do think TV is part of the trouble.'

And Mac suddenly remembers how, on TV, when cops say, 'Don't worry,' they are *every time* proved wrong.

Beyond the beam of the police car lights the reserve is a restless inky black. Mac's mouth is dry. Shane McKinnon shines his police-issue torch into the boot and Mac peers over his shoulder.

'I don't get it.' His voice is hoarse. 'Why would they leave it here? And where's Ginny?'

'My guess,' says Shane, 'is she'll be waiting when you get home.'

He unlocks the boot of the police car. 'Okay with you if I take that TV back to the station?'

Mac helps the cop transfer it from one car boot to the other. Who, he wonders, would steal a TV as old and ugly as this?

He doesn't believe that Ginny will be back home waiting. He suspects the policeman's judgement has been clouded by the Michelle–Beverley connection. Shane is probably convinced that Ginny, too, has done a runner; that somehow Mac has that effect on women.

So Mac says very firmly that they must take Shane's torch and search the dark corners of the reserve. Shane shrugs, then leads the way, and in the light's beam, ferns, tree trunks, milkshake containers and a couple of used condoms spring to life.

'Remember those magic painting books?' Shane says. 'You just added water and bingo, the colours were there.'

Mac thinks that isn't the kind of thing he'd go saying if he was a cop. But he likes Shane the better for having said it.

'Happier now?' asks Shane when every shadow has been explored.

Mac has a picture of Ginny somewhere above them, her body wedged between branches, but how can he suggest that they start over again, beaming skyward?

'If you haven't heard anything in, say, a couple of hours give us a bell,' the cop says.

226

9.15 Harriet finds out more than she needs to know and Mac is getting desperate.

Jed has finally fallen asleep and, any other night, Harriet would be reading or listening to the radio — possibly both at once — and feeling happy because this was *her* time and hers alone. But tonight she frets and paces. Tonight, had Ginny not been so totally bloody selfish Harriet could be engrossed in *Ruth is worried about her stomach pains and John and Sarah are further estranged* or *Jarod matches wits with a group of students* or *Prue's dreams are filled with images of a strange man.*

When the phone rings she snatches it up, but it's only Lisa, mother of Charlton.

'This may seem a strange question,' says Lisa, 'but your friend with the nose rings . . .'

'Something's happened?'

'I just wondered if she was at home tonight?'

'I wish. I need to get hold of . . .'

'I know where she is.' Lisa sounding so pleased with herself. 'She's here. Booked in for a night with some bloke. Only she gave us a phoney name. If you want I could put you through.'

'No,' says Harriet. Now that she knows, she's happy to wait. 'Thanks, Lisa, but it doesn't matter.'

There's a silence.

'Okay. Gotta go now,' says Lisa, and hangs up in Harriet's ear.

Harriet goes over the conversation to see if she inadvertently dropped Ginny in it. She knows that her friend is worried about nosy parkers getting her benefit cut off. All the same, she feels a bit resentful. No one's ever given Harriet a slap-up night in a motel. Somehow it doesn't seem right — renting a bed when you already have one only three or four ks away. Not when the state is paying you.

227

Mac and his Cortina have done a slow crawl up and down every street. His cellphone is on, the light on his answerphone waits for him, unblinking. He thinks he'll have to go back to the reserve, look up in those trees, but he's putting it off. Ginny has a raggedy-doll look and he knows the fate of raggedy dolls, has seen enough of them in the local tip with their leaking seams and partially severed limbs.

10.00 Ginny reflects on balance.

Ginny wakes to the flickering light of the TV and a room she has nothing to do with. The boy Corin has fallen asleep on top of the duvet. The bedside clock tells her she's slept no more than a hour. Corin must have changed channels — men with guns pop up like sideshow rabbits, shoot, then disappear. Ginny can feel herself smiling. She remembers how the Group used to talk about *balance. You're aiming for balance. We all need balance.*

Well, Ginny's just put her life on one end of the seesaw and dropped a shitload of bricks on the other. Everything's flying about in the air and it feels great. Feels, in fact, like she's been underwater holding her breath for at least two years and now she's surfacing.

10.30 Harriet needs to make a decision.

On his way back from the reserve Mac calls in at Harriet's place. He's been thinking about why Harriet was needing to get in touch with Ginny on this particular night. Whatever the reason, he needs to know. Besides, he doesn't want to go home and be there alone.

Harriet comes out when she hears the car. 'Oh, brilliant,' she says. 'At last!'

Mac is confused. Ginny's here then?'

It takes a few moments to get this sorted out and for Mac to explain about the TV being in the hands of the police.

'I'll take you to get it. Right now if you want,' says Mac.

Harriet declines because of Jed being asleep and she offers to make Mac a cup of tea. She's tempted to suggest he could go to the police station on his own but it might be unwise to consign her TV once again to that Cortina.

She feels sorry for Mac. He's in a terrible state.

'I've looked all over,' he mumbles into his oversized hands.

Harriet doesn't know what to say. After all, it's nothing to do with her, none of it is. She should not have to be the one to tell him. And she's Ginny's friend, not Mac's. And there's always more to this kind of thing than meets the eye.

'I guess she's told you about Beverley?' he tests, weighing the sodden tea bag on the raised spoon. 'How she took off?'

'Only . . . briefly.' But amusingly.

'It's the job,' he says. 'Too much away from home. Women don't like being left on their own. Isn't that right?'

Harriet gives it some thought. 'I wouldn't mind,' she says. 'Some women might think it's the best of both worlds.'

If she doesn't tell him soon she won't be able to tell him at all because she would then have to explain why she hadn't told him right away.

Perhaps they'll mount a search — policemen and dogs and volunteers — all for nothing.

What's the right thing to do? How is she supposed to decide?

She'll look for a sign. If Mac stirs his sugar clockwise she'll tell him where to find Ginny.

But Jed now comes to join them, blue pyjama'd and sweet with sleep. He remembers Mac. 'You come in your truck?'

'Next time,' says Mac. 'I promise.'

Jed smiles at Harriet as he drapes himself over Mac's knee.

Mac forgets about sugar. He takes off his cap and drops it over the little boy's head. It covers him right to his mouth and ears. Jed laughs.

In front of Jed's eyes is an arm fluffy with fur, all of it going in one direction as if a big wind has been blowing. But when Jed reaches out to touch that fur he feels only the crinkled skin beneath.

If he tips his head right back he can see his mother's face, the way she's watching him with her mouth soft at the corners.